Love in the Outback

SUSAN HORSNELL
INTERNATIONAL BEST SELLING AUTHOR

GW00503474

Author of Amazon No 1 Best Sellers in 2018:

Matt – Book 1 in The Carter Brothers Series

Clay – Book 3 in The Carter Brothers Series

No 1 Amazon Best Seller in February 2019:

Andrew's Outback Love – Book 1 in The Outback
Australia Series

No 1 Amazon Best Seller on Release July 2019

Ruby's Outback Love – Book 2 in The Outback
Australia Series

No 1 Amazon Best Seller in May 2019:

Eight Letters

Contents:

LOVE IN THE OUTBACK

Written by Susan Horsnell

Edited by Word Writer Pro and Margaret Tanner

Line Edited and Proofread by Robyn Corcoran

Cover Design by Tara from Fantasia Frog Designs:

https://www.facebook.com/groups/155616269 7844738/

Note to Reader:

This book is purely fictional, a product of the author's imagination and is written for the reader's enjoyment. It is not intended to be used for Historical or Practical education.

Some characters, although real have been given fictional names, the towns and businesses mentioned are real and information has been sourced from notes after my visits. At the time of my visit, the information was accurate.

I would like to thank the people and businesses of Longreach for this storyline and strongly recommend a visit to this fascinating town.

This book is written in **Australian** English.

About the Author

I live in sunny Queensland, Australia and retired after 37 years of Nursing.

My husband of 45 years, together with our elderly Jack Russell Terrier and extremely opinionated 26-year-old Cockatiel, enjoy exploring the country with our caravan.

When we are at home, which is a small rural village, we spend our time renovating our home.

I write a variety of stories including Western Historical Romance, Contemporary Romance, Male/Male, Ménage and Shapeshifter.

Each book has a strong focus on story line with romantic interest building throughout.

I explore real life issues from kids on the streets to motorcycle war and put my own twist on each one.

Author Links

Blog: http://susanhorsnell.com

Web:
http://www.susanhorsnellromanceauthor.com/

Facebook:
https://www.facebook.com/susanhorsnellroma
nceauthor/

Bookbub:
https://www.bookbub.com/profile/susan-
horsnell

Newsletter: http://bit.ly/2t5INNB

CHAPTER ONE

EMMALYNNE

I strutted the catwalk in a ridiculous creation by a supposed fashion designer for the last time. Camera flashes popped, lighting up the venue like fireworks in the night sky.

"Emma, this way, honey!"

"Emma, over here, darlin'!"

I gritted my teeth and held my signature smile in place. Most models preferred a downtrodden look, the smile was what set me apart.

Ten years I'd been gracing the catwalks of London, Paris, Milan, Melbourne and here – my hometown, Sydney.

Ten years of wearing ridiculous outfits for close to insane designers. Did they really think any of their outlandish clothes would be worn by normal people on the street?

Ten years of being called Emma instead of my fucking name – Emmalynne. I hadn't given anyone permission to shorten it but they did it regardless. Even my parents, brother and extended family only ever called me by my full name.

The date was March 3rd 2016. A date I would forever consider the day of my freedom. The day I had taken my future into my own hands. I would no longer be dictated to by anyone.

My agent - Sally, manager – Brett, designers and fashion show organizers had pleaded, begged, cajoled and even offered me insane amounts of money to continue. But at twenty-seven years old, I was done. Finished with it all.

I smiled down at my parents, brother – Craig, who was four years older than me and sister in law – Marley, who were seated in the front row. As soon as I was done, we had a celebratory dinner planned at my brother's home in Wahroonga. As much as I would have loved to take them to a fancy restaurant for dinner, I knew the paparazzi would be swarming all over us and there wouldn't be a moments peace. It wouldn't have been fair to my family, other diners or restaurant staff.

The public announcement of my retirement had been left until a few hours before the show began. I was sure the people I dealt with were convinced I'd change my mind, that I was merely having a diva moment.

It stung to know they might think of me as a diva, I had never given them any cause to believe it. I had prided myself on both my professional and private behavior. I had never behaved like a spoiled brat or thrown a tantrum in all my working life.

The fact I was calling it quits made headline news everywhere, a red banner announcing 'breaking news' was spread across screens on both television and the internet. I found it unbelievable, I was a fucking model for God's sake, I hadn't taken part in some heroic feat.

I was paid ludicrous amounts of money to wear clothes, the designers and manufacturer's hoping someone would buy them. As I said earlier, no one in their right mind could wear half of what I was forced to parade in. I most certainly wouldn't. Give me jeans, a t-shirt and joggers any day.

Since I was seventeen years old and won my first modelling contract, I'd been raised up and put on a pedestal because I was long-legged and pretty. Young girls admired me, they had no idea how vicious the industry could be, how it had ruined many good lives. Nope, I just didn't get it.

On the positive side, the money had enabled me to contribute to some very worthy animal charities – Animals Asia being my favourite. I had visited and seen the work being done by the charities, they made a big difference in the lives of the animals they helped.

Animals were my passion and in the near future I planned to open a sanctuary, to give the animals who needed it a home, refuge.

I turned and headed back down the runway, when I glanced down at my family again, Mum smiled back at me and gave me a slight nod. Dad beamed with pride as did my brother and his wife.

My family were my rock. Sanity in a world of insanity and I couldn't wait to be able to spend more time with them.

Shouts continued, accompanied by continual flashes as I made my way back to where Gerard, the designer stood waiting. When I reached him, he palmed his hands on my face and kissed my cheeks. He was one of the nice people even if his designs tended to be on the wacky side.

"I'll miss you sweet girl, but you don't belong in this industry. You have far too pure a soul."

Tears pricked my eyes and I hugged him. "Thank you, Gerard."

I turned and faced the audience for the last time. Flashes popped like a machine gun being discharged. I waved to everyone, blew a kiss, shouted out my thanks, squeezed Gerard's hand and headed for the dressing room.

***

I sat before the mirror, brushed my long, burgundy coloured waves and pinned them up at the sides.

My thoughts travelled back to last month.....

My one true friend since our school days had been Nicole. She had died in a fiery crash on the Sydney Harbor Bridge four weeks earlier. A drunk driver had veered out of his lane, collided with Nicole and flipped her vehicle. It had exploded immediately, there had been no chance of anyone getting her free.

I'd been devastated when mum had phoned to tell me and it was the catalyst for me to make the decision I had been wrestling with for so long.

Nicole had been a high-powered banker and like me, she wasn't in a relationship or married. She'd insisted she was wedded to her career. My friend had always been there for me when I'd returned home from a show overseas. She gave me a place to regroup and the space to get my head back on straight. She'd been my safe harbour two years before when Josh had broken up with me while I was in London.

We'd been together for three years and I'd been stupid enough to think it would last forever. Josh proved to be insecure and, in the end, he was unable to deal with other men ogling his girlfriend. I decided after the heartbreak the split caused, I would stay single while I remained a model. There was far too much travel in my career and it wouldn't have been fair to either of us. I also couldn't have the animals I craved which had been a major factor when I'd considered walking away.

I'd flown home from Milan for Nicole's funeral. It broke my heart knowing my beautiful friend, so full of life and vigor, was no more. The organizers had objected to postponing the show, I was their star attraction and I think they were worried I wouldn't return. I was annoyed they would think I could let them down and didn't hesitate to tell them so. I also stated they could sue me for every penny I was worth, it would have made no difference. I was attending the funeral and what they decided was up to them.

They grudgingly relented and apologized for their insensitivity. When the announcement was made that the show was postponed because I needed to fly back to Australia for a few days to attend a funeral, messages of sympathy poured in.

The outpouring of grief was overwhelming but didn't surprise me. Nicole was a person who had made friends easily and was loyal to a fault. Many of her friends were like me, they had been with her since we'd first started school. While I had drifted away from the others because of the travel, Nicole had remained good friends with us all.

There hadn't been a dry eye at the service, even big, macho men had shed tears over her loss. All of my family had attended, it was never doubted that my parents would fly down from the property they had bought five years earlier, fifty kilometres from Longreach in Queensland.

Craig and Marley had been by my side while our parents supported Nicole's devastated mum and dad – Evan and Melanie. She'd been their only child and the loss for them was unbearable. They flew out to Longreach with mum and dad the following day. Mum said they could grieve privately, surrounded by the healing hand of nature.

I'd never been to the property, my parents had always elected to come down and visit me in Sydney, stating they could visit my brother at the same time. I looked forward to becoming an outback gal, I certainly wouldn't miss the lights and noise of the city.

***

After swiping a layer of nude coloured lipstick on, I stood, grabbed my bag and glanced around for the last time. My heart felt light. I was finally free!

I stepped outside the room to find a few of the other models I'd worked with over the years. Brett and Sally stood off to one side with Gerard and the organizer in charge of the Sydney show.

One by one, flowers and gifts were pushed into my arms and I received hugs, kisses and well-wishes. I was surprised to see many of them shed tears.

I thanked them all, although many had been good to me, I had never regarded them as friends. Sally and Brett took the flowers and gifts, assuring me they would deliver them to my brother's home later in the evening.

After one final goodbye, I headed for a side door in the building where I knew my parents would be waiting outside. I smiled at the security guard manning the door, he returned my smile and pushed the door open.

"Good luck, Emmalynne."

"Thank you."

I stepped into the night to see dad's hire car parked a few steps away. Dad had been standing waiting by the door, I saw mum was in the front passenger seat.

Flashes lit up the night, photos were being hurriedly snapped by those held back by security tape with the added muscle of guards.

Dad held my elbow and guided me to the car, opened the door and after I climbed in, he closed it again. After rounding the car, he slid behind the wheel and started the engine. I breathed a sigh of relief.

"I knew it would be crazy when word got out I was done, but that was nuts. It was like I was a movie star or something, I have no idea what they see in me."

Dad turned onto a road I knew led to the airport, we were headed away from my brother's home in Wahroonga.

"Where are we going?"

Mum turned in her seat and looked back at me.

Craig called to say there are reporters and photographers everywhere at his place. He contacted the hotel where we're staying and they agreed to set up a private room so we could have dinner there."

"Mum…" I suspected this might be a cover for a farewell party.

"I promise you, sweetheart, I haven't organized a surprise end of modelling party, not that I didn't want to. You said you only wanted your family and I have respected your decision."

"Thank you. I want to spend some time with Craig and Marley before we leave in the morning."

Mum turned back to face the front and dad spoke.

"The reason people are all over you, darlin', is because you're beautiful inside and out. You don't party, do drugs or drink. You show people that regardless of what is going on around you, you can choose to be a good person. I'm so very proud of you."

Dad's words brought tears to my eyes. "You're biased, dad."

"Maybe a little but I speak the truth."

He turned the car into the hotel and eased it up to the front door. We stepped out and dad handed the keys to the valet for parking. Only a few paparazzi hung around, it seemed most thought we would go back to Craig's.

Dad ushered mum and I inside and waved at the man who stood behind the reception desk.

They had checked in earlier in the day, acquiring adjoining rooms for them and me. The man immediately strode towards us.

"Follow me, sir. The room is ready, your son and his wife are already here."

We thanked him as he led us to an elevator, away from prying eyes who were being carefully watched by two guards at the entrance. They were big men who stood with their legs spread and arms crossed over broad chests, daring anyone to approach.

I knew the media would eventually give up and go away, my name would vanish from the news and I would become a has-been. I looked forward to when the day came that I could enter a store on my own and not be recognized.

CHAPTER TWO

We entered a large room in time to see a waiter place drinks in front of Craig and Marley. When he noticed us, he approached and enquired as to what drinks we would like. I requested my usual – lemon, lime and bitters. Mum ordered a gin sling and dad, being a true-blue Aussie, ordered a beer.

Once the orders had been taken, we took our seats at the table, I sat opposite my big brother and his wife. He reached over the table to squeeze my hand before taking a swig of beer straight from the bottle – like father, like son – all class.

"Sorry it couldn't be at our place, sis, but I didn't want people trampling Marley's garden or peering through the windows while we were trying to eat. I guessed you could do with the break from their prying. Oh, and Brett and Sally dropped in all the flowers and gifts. We asked at reception for someone to put them in your room."

The drinks we'd ordered were placed on the table and I sipped at mine before speaking.

"I completely understand and thank you. I hope they don't follow me to Longreach. They should know by now, I'm not giving them anything about my private life. I mean which part of private don't they understand? I just want to be left alone."

"What you have to put up with in your life would drive me crazy, sis. I don't know how you've put up with it for so long."

"Ex-life," I stated firmly.

"Will you miss it?" Marley asked.

"Not at all, which I suppose is sad in some ways. The travel, exotic cities, bright lights, people – none of it. No, I'm well and truly ready to take dad up on his offer. I'm going to buy fifty acres in the southern corner of the property like we discussed. The river runs through part of the plot which will be perfect for the animal sanctuary I plan to build."

Dad shook his finger at me. "I said I would give you and your brother some land when you were ready. There was never any mention of you paying for it. Put the money towards the buildings you need."

"It doesn't seem fair, dad."

"I can't see how, I've offered Craig the same. The whole lot will belong to both of you after I'm gone anyway."

"Don't talk that way Christopher, we all need you around for a lot longer yet." Mum kissed his cheek.

"As long as you're sure, dad, I could certainly use the extra money for the animals."

"Having my little girl living so close is payment enough for me. Now I just need to convince those two." Dad nodded his head in the direction of Craig and his wife.

"I can't wait to get there and explore the town. It will be so good to be a nobody at last."

Dad grinned. "Sweetheart, you'll never be a nobody but Longreach is certainly different to anywhere else you've been. The town is suffering terribly from the drought. We've been fortunate, we can afford to buy in feed thanks to the money we made from selling the place in Wahroonga. It enabled us to buy the property with plenty left over to invest and keep us going in the tough times."

"How about the neighbours?" I knew mum and dad pretty much lived in the middle of nowhere, but they did have one neighbour who was close by.

According to dad, the neighbour had his home on the other side of the river which formed the boundary between the two properties. It was in the same area as the land I was going to build on. When the river was dry, like it was at the moment, dad said the cattle wandered from one side to the other but neither man minded. It was swings and roundabouts, his cattle ate some of dad's grain, dad's cattle ate the other man's grain.

My parents didn't say much about him, I didn't even know his name. Apparently, he'd been a country boy all his life and had bought his property about ten years earlier. Dad said he'd been extremely helpful with teaching him the ins and outs of how to manage and run his lifelong dream .

When mum had called me to say they'd sold their home and were moving onto a cattle station, it hadn't surprised me. Dad had talked about his lifelong dream of owning property in the country for as long as I could remember.

My parents had visited numerous areas, but they'd fallen in love with Longreach and its people and the decision was made to buy there.

I studied dad's face as he gave the waiter our dinner order, we'd designated him the one in charge after making our choices.

His skin was now a golden brown due to him spending so much time in the outdoors. Quite different from the pale skin we were used to when he was confined behind a desk or in a courtroom in his former profession as a lawyer. His blue eyes sparkled with a relaxed happiness. The stress lines which had marred his face for years were now barely visible. As with my mother, the change in lifestyle had taken years off the way they looked and acted. They seemed somehow invigorated.

Once the order was given, dad returned to our previous topic of conversation.

"Tom Addison is struggling. The Outback Angels have been providing feed for both his animals and family. I spoke with him in town a few days ago and he said he's got a couple of years at most if the drought persists. Pete Wheeler and John Morcombe have both walked away from their properties. I knew Pete would toss it in when his dad committed suicide over their situation."

"It's so very sad, if only there was some way to make it rain."

Dad laughed at my comment. "You'd be a millionaire many times over if you could figure that out."

"How is your nearest neighbour fairing?"

"Nick Johnson?"

"Is that the name of the man on the other side of the river?"

"Yes, hadn't I told you before now?"

"Nope, he was always – our neighbour or him."

Dad laughed. "It's only taken five years then, huh?"

"I guess I never really thought to ask, we had so many other things to discuss when we saw each other."

"Well, Nick's pretty wealthy from what I hear and can see for myself. He's been helping out a lot of the locals in one way or another. It's a fine line as to what we can do because we don't want to trample all over their pride."

"Where did his money come from?" Yeah, I was nosy, I'd never die wondering.

Dad shook his head and swigged at his beer. "No idea although there are a few rumours – gold strike, opal strike, lottery win. No one knows. Country people enjoy their gossip, but they don't pry into another man's business. Bit of an oxymoron, actually. Nick's a good man and a damn good neighbour."

Meals were placed before us and I inhaled the delicious aromas of Chicken Chasseur with a serving of mashed potato and buttered beans. My mouth watered in anticipation. I picked up the knife and fork, cut into the perfectly cooked chicken and popped the piece, along with mushroom and a generous dollop of sauce, into my mouth. It tasted as delicious as it smelled, and I moaned as the different taste sensations erupted on my tongue. The rest of my family laughed before also getting stuck into their choices.

Conversation flowed throughout dinner, discussions about my latest trips to London and Milan, more talk of the drought and Craig discussed his and Marley's plans to travel overseas for a couple of years. That didn't make any of us particularly happy, but we understood their desire to see the world before settling down and raising a family. Mum despaired, that at the rate we were both going, she'd never be a Nanna.

Once we'd finished eating, we relaxed back in our chairs and sipped on our second round of drinks while waiting for coffee.

"I have no idea where you put all the food you eat, Emmalynne. If I ate like you do, people would mistake me for being a beached whale."

I laughed at Marley's complaint. I'd heard the same words many times before. I was tall and slender, a long way from what was considered skinny and model material. When I'd begun modelling, I'd been ordered to diet, or take drugs because I was far too big to ever become a success.

I'd stated with a will of steel, instilled in me by my parents, that I was perfect as I was and if they couldn't accept me as I was, then I didn't want a career in the industry.

I'd come close to not having one. Jobs had been few and far between in the beginning because I was considered too big. Big equalled healthy and didn't appear to be the look designers wanted. I hadn't backed down and gave myself six months to make a comfortable living before finding a different career.

I attended the jobs I was given, always on time and did what was asked of me in a professional, dedicated manner. I also decided I was not going to be like the other models and look miserable when I paraded on the catwalk.

Audiences took a liking to me, they liked my natural curves and my smile. Designers talked amongst themselves about how I was a pleasure to work with. I was neither temperamental or difficult. My career sky-rocketed. Jobs poured in – most I'd had to refuse because I couldn't be in two places at once, but I always wrote a personal note explaining why I'd declined. Over the years, many had asked again and when there wasn't a clash of dates, I'd happily accepted.

I had two hard and fast rules during my career – one – I never charged, or allowed my agency to charge, for my modelling or helping out at a charitable group event. Two – my family always came first. If something happened to one of them and I needed to go home, it was understood I would be on the first plane. Shows would never take priority. Fortunately, the only time I'd had to enforce rule number two was when Nicole had passed away.

I sipped at the steaming coffee before me and commented on Marley's statement.

"I have been blessed with good genes, Marley."

"Thanks to your father." Mum glanced at dad. "He's like a human beanpole regardless of what he shoves in his mouth."

Mum was still a beautiful woman and many people remarked I was the image of her. She was tall and slender but since hitting the age of sixty, she'd developed a slight pot belly as had my father.

"Mum, if I look half as good as you at your age, I'll be very happy. You really are gorgeous."

Dad hugged mum around the waist and pulled her towards him before kissing her cheek.

"I agree with our daughter, Willow, you are gorgeous and I'm one hell of a lucky man."

Mum brushed her lips over dads. "I'm one hell of a lucky woman."

Love shone from their eyes as they gazed at each other. I could only hope that one day I'd find the same kind of love, but I wouldn't count on it to happen any time soon.

***

It was after eleven-thirty by the time we said goodnight and goodbye to Craig and Marley. They left to go home, promising to visit Longreach in the next couple of months. Mum and dad escorted me to my room and after giving them a hug and kiss, I slipped inside, locking the door behind me.

The room resembled a florist's store, I resolved to speak to reception the following morning to have them sent out to an old people's home. I was sure they would brighten their day.

Although I was tired, I was far too wound up and excited to sleep. I sat on the bed and rummaged through the gifts – designer earrings and clutch purses – God only knew what I would do with a clutch purse in the outback, but it was a lovely gesture just the same. There was sexy lingerie from one of the designers I'd modeled for, a couple of my favourite authors' books and a couple of pretty crystal statuettes. They were all gifts I could easily put into my suitcase.

I placed them off to one side, kicked off my shoes and padded through to the adjoining bathroom. After removing my makeup, I took a shower, luxuriating in the warm water flowing over my aching joints, dried off and dressed in a pair of sleep shorts and tank top. After grabbing my laptop, I sat cross-legged on the bed and began checking emails. There were hundreds, it would take days to answer them all, so I shut down, packed the device into my bag and crossed to the large wall of windows.

Pulling the curtains aside revealed the lights of Sydney Domestic Airport below, runways clearly visible. Aircraft were parked at the end of the boarding and departure bridges, probably done for the day.

Tomorrow morning, my parents and I would be down there getting ready to board our first flight to Brisbane. After a two hour layover, we'd then board the Qantaslink aircraft which would take us to Longreach – a two hour flight. It would take us the better part of the day before we arrived at our destination. Greg, dad's foreman would pick us up at the airport and from there we would be driven out to the property, fifty kilometres away. Excitement bubbled inside, I couldn't wait to begin this new phase of my life.

I gazed off to the north, towards the city. Lights of all colours glittered and sparkled, but there were few stars visible overhead. Even though the night was clear, smog and lights prevented most from being seen. I wondered what the night sky in my new town would be like.

CHAPTER THREE

The arrivals gate and airport at Longreach were certainly very different from any others I'd been in. I supposed it was typical of most regional airports.

Dad's foreman, Greg Williams, who had been with him from the time the property had been purchased, waited at the arrivals gate. Once we'd moved clear and were no longer in anyone's way, dad introduced me.

"Greg, this is our daughter, Emmalynne. Sweetheart, this is the man who held down the fort every time we came to see you."

Greg offered his hand and I shook. "Pleased to meet you, Greg and thank you for keeping things going so mum and dad could visit with me."

"It was my pleasure, darlin'. Your photos don't do you justice. You'll turn a few heads here that's for sure."

Greg had a smile which caused his eyes to narrow and it lit up his face. It was obvious he smiled a lot if the creases at the sides of his mouth and eyes were any indication.

He was around the same age as dad – late fifties/early sixties. Where dad was tall and lean, Greg was slightly shorter and more muscled. His skin had a sun-bronzed leathery appearance, thanks to having spent his life on the land. His blue eyes danced with life. Thick, dark hair was threaded with gray, the flattened appearance was no doubt due to always wearing a hat.

After our meeting, he headed in the direction which signs indicated was the baggage collection area. I smiled at his swagger as I followed with mum. It was obvious he spent a great deal of time on horseback if his bow-legged walk was any indication.

As mum and I stayed close behind, Greg gave dad an update about the property and they discussed several things. They might as well have been speaking a foreign language, the only thing I understood was the fact cattle were scheduled for the sale yards in the following few days.

I switched off and glanced around at my surroundings, there wasn't much to be seen. A few people glanced at me and smiled as we passed by.

While we waited at the carousel for our luggage, several people glanced furtively in my direction. I didn't mind, none of them infringed on my privacy.

I had brought only two suitcases. The furniture from my apartment, along with other personal items I didn't want to part with, were being brought up by road and placed into storage until I built a place of my own.

With the luggage collected, we followed the signs towards the carpark. As soon as I stepped through the door, the searing heat hit me with the force of a battering ram. Hadn't anyone informed the place it was now autumn?

Greg and dad jammed hats on their heads. Mum handed me a pink baseball cap with the word *Longreach* embroidered across the front. I pulled it onto my head and dug sunglasses from my bag. When mum also pulled one on, I burst into laughter. Never in my life had I expected to see my mother wearing a baseball cap. Her style was more formal.

"Is it always so hot?" It must have been well over 100 degrees and it was now well after three in the afternoon.

"Shoot, this isn't hot. You wait until summer, even the flies are too hot to bother you then."

I laughed at the image which jumped into my mind at Greg's words.

"What's so funny now?" Mum asked as we weaved in and out of vehicles in the carpark.

"I was picturing hot flies sitting back with a cold drink by a pool."

Dad turned back and laughed at me. "I see you have retained your weird sense of humour."

The rest of us laughed with him.

When we neared a large white dual cab ute which was more like a small truck, Greg pushed a button on the remote in his hand. Lights flashed, along with a cheeping sound. Mum and I approached the back doors while our luggage was lifted into the rear tray.

"You driving, Chris?" Greg held the keys in the air.

"No, I'll leave it to you, it's been a long day."

Mum and I slipped into the back seat while the men climbed into the front.

We left the car park and Greg turned the truck onto the highway. He picked up speed as we headed south.

While my parents and Greg continued catching up on local news, I took in the surroundings. The area was flat and as dad had warned, it was extremely dry. There was next to no feed on the ground. I was dismayed by the large numbers of kangaroos which lay dead on the side of the roads, probably on the move for desperately needed water.

The kilometres passed by in a blur of sameness and before long I found myself dozing. When the clicking of an indicator echoed in the cab and the vehicle slowed, my eyes flashed open.

"Are we there already?"

Dad chuckled at my question. "No, just turning into our driveway."

We turned onto a dirt road and when I glanced back it was to see red dust billowing behind us.

"How far is it to the house, dad?"

"About twenty kilometres."

"You have a twenty-kilometre driveway? How do you check the mail and put the rubbish bin out?"

Dad turned in his seat to face me. "Mick and Rusty normally pick it up and put it in their truck before they go drinking. It's normally at least once a week. Most of the rubbish we burn, but what we can't is taken to the refuse centre every couple of weeks."

"Wow, you really are in the middle of nowhere. I didn't know there was anywhere that people didn't get a mail pickup or rubbish service."

Dad turned back around and mum patted my hand. "You have no idea sweetheart."

I laid my head against the back of the seat and sighed with contentment.

***

Greg slowed the ute to a stop in front of a colonial style home, typical of what was found in the outback. It was painted in a soft blue, the window surroundings, roof and trim were bright white. It was postcard perfect.

A huge windmill stood nearby, another iconic outback structure, the blades reaching out into the air.

When I stepped from the truck, the *thunk thunk* as they turned could be heard along with the low whir of a motor.

Off to one side were various outbuildings, painted the same as the home. Dad would no doubt show me through the buildings over the following few days.

I grabbed one of my suitcases from where Greg had placed it on the ground and headed to the steps leading onto the verandah which ran the full width of the house. The metallic roof was supported by large white painted posts. A love swing, small tables and comfy looking chairs were placed at various intervals on the highly polished floors. Several fold back doors were spaced along the length. Once open, the outside and inside would become one.

I could picture myself spending many an evening, sitting and watching the splendid outback sunset.

***

The home inside was as stunning as I'd expected. Wooden furniture complimented both the style of home and location. The place was flooded with light thanks to the fold back glass doors. Pale blue chintz curtains fluttered in a breeze supplied by an overhead fan which spun slowly. Polished rosewood floors had an almost mirror finish. The photographs mum had sent of both inside and outside, had not done the place justice.

"I can't believe I haven't been here before now. I would never have left if I had."

"I suspected that would happen which is why your dad and I always insisted on coming to Sydney for Christmas and holidays. It gave us a chance to catch up with the rest of the family and prevented you from giving your career up before you were ready."

"I wondered why you were so adamant about me not visiting. You were right, if I had come here before now, I wouldn't have gone back to modelling. This is a dream come true, mum."

"Come in the kitchen, it's exactly as we talked about."

I kissed her cheek, left my suitcase in the living room and followed mum.

The kitchen was enormous and everything was exactly as we'd discussed. There were a multitude of cupboards in light pine coloured wood, complimented by rustic brass handles. Stainless steel, state of the art appliances shone in the sunlight. Benchtops were white granite with matching tiled splash backs.

In the centre of the room was a pine wooden table surrounded by six chairs. It was identical to how I envisaged the kitchen of my own home.

"I love this, it's perfect and so big."

"Dad knocked out the dining room wall and made this one large room. It made more sense, you know we didn't use the dining room in our last place."

"Yes, it makes sense. I think when I build my place, I'll have one large great room."

"It's really all you need, sweetheart."

I stepped over to the large window above the sink and peered out at the view. Pastures were dotted with cattle gathered around feeding troughs. The sun was beginning to slip to the horizon – pinks purples and oranges, lit up the sky in a kaleidoscope of colour.

Mum moved up beside me and wrapped an arm around my waist. I leaned my head against her shoulder.

She kissed my cheek. "I'm glad you're here, I felt like we'd lost you for the past ten years."

"You never lost me, mum."

"I know. Come and I'll show you your room."

We backtracked through the living room, I grabbed a suitcase and followed mum down the hallway. She stopped and pushed open the door before standing aside.

I entered a room tastefully decorated in lemon and white – lemon was my favourite colour.

The wood theme was continued in the room with a large queen-sized bed, matching side tables and chest of drawers. The carpet was pale lemon, the curtains a slightly darker shade.

"You have a walk-in robe and your own bathroom."

Mum pointed out two white painted doors pushed one open and flipped on the light. I peeked inside to see a walk-in shower, white fittings and cabinetry, lemon towels and accessories.

"I love it."

Mum closed the door and moved to the wall of curtains, she pulled one aside. "These doors are retractable so you can go onto the verandah. It's very light and bright in here during the day."

"I can see myself sitting out there with a drink and book."

"I'd probably join you, but for now, I'll leave you to unpack. Come down to the kitchen when you've had enough, I'm going to get a start on dinner."

"I can help, you've had a long day."

"No, get yourself unpacked. Your father will be in shortly and he'll help if need be, he loves to cook these days."

"Where is he?"

"Out helping Greg bed the place down – checking sheds are closed and the orphaned calves are settled for the night. One of the men will feed them during the night. We keep everything closed up to keep out foxes and wild dogs."

"How many calves are there?"

"Six at the moment."

Six babies without mummas, my heart hurt for them. I couldn't wait to see them the following day.

"Rusty and Mick feed them during the day and night, sometimes I help out if I'm not too busy. They have to be bottle fed every six hours."

"They must be so cute."

"They are. It's sad we lost their mothers, but they have each other for company which helps. Pilot stays in the barn with them at night for extra protection in case something does get in."

"Pilot?"

"One of the dogs. We have four and before you decide on bringing them inside and spoiling them, you need to know they are working dogs and stay in kennels. Kennels with state of the art heating, cooling, beds and piped music."

"Wow, way to spoil them, mum. What breed are they?"

"Pilot and King are Border Collies, Zipper and Pete are Kelpies."

"Do you have cats?"

"Three barn cats and they stay in the barn where feed is kept. They keep the rodents out. Don't even think about bringing them indoors."

I pouted, mum knew me too well.

"It's a working property, sweetheart. The dogs and cats are fed well, have a weekly bath – the dogs that is, heaven knows we'd end up shredded if we attempted to bath the cats. When it's hot and chores are done, the dogs often go swimming with Mick and Rusty down at the river. The animals here are well loved and get a lot of affection. They also get the best veterinary care from Laura Adams in town. Your dad wouldn't have it any other way."

"I can believe it, I know how much he loves animals. I know how much you both do."

"Pilot idolizes your dad and follows him everywhere."

"I can't wait to see them."

"Well, this isn't getting dinner done, I'll leave you to it."

I waited for mum to leave the room, hefted the suitcase onto my bed and began the tedious job of unpacking. After living my life out of a suitcase for so many years, it would be great to actually settle in one place.

CHAPTER FOUR

The following day dawned bright and sunny. After showering and dressing, I pulled back the curtains, folded the doors back and stepped out onto the verandah.

I had never been one for sleeping in and the colours of an early dawn still decorated the sky. The sun sat on the horizon, promising another scorching hot day. There wasn't a cloud in the sky which was good for me, but not so good for the area.

The lowing of cattle floated in on the slight breeze. Birds chirped and fussed, high up in a melaleuca tree. Brolgas strutted about on the lawn – there were two larger birds and what appeared to be three smaller juveniles. They were completely engrossed in a small plastic pool of water someone had placed in one corner of the garden.

Mum loved to garden and she had done a superb job of planning this one. I assumed the plants had been selected for their tolerance to drought. I didn't recognize many, I was a long way from being a plant connoisseur, but I did notice there was a large variety of acacias which would bring the birds in.

Hearing movement in the kitchen, I made my way there. Dad was seated at the table, eating toast and checking the news on his iPad. Mum was reading a magazine she'd picked up at the airport while she drank a cup of tea.

I kissed them both on the cheek. "Morning."

"Morning, love. Help yourself to breakfast, cereals are on the bench top near the toaster and there is extra toast here on the table. The coffee pot only needs hot water."

"Thanks, mum."

While helping myself to a bowl of Just Right cereal, I boiled the kettle and filled the small coffee pot. I was the only person who drank coffee, the rest of my family drank tea. I placed my breakfast on the table and sat beside mum.

"What are you both up to today?" I spread margarine and strawberry jam on a piece of toast and took a bite.

"I have a spot of cleaning to do and the washing we brought back from Sydney." Mum poured herself another cup of tea.

"I'm going to be flat out getting the cattle ready. The truck will be here at six in the morning to take them to the sale yards in town. I can't spend much time with you over the next couple of days, so you'll be left to your own devices I'm afraid."

"I understand, dad. Who will be feeding the calves?"

"Mick will be starting with them in about half an hour. Go down and introduce yourself, I'm sure he'd appreciate your help."

"I'd love to help out. How old are the calves?"

"Between six days and three weeks. Our bull calf is struggling, he's not feeding well at all. Mick was talking about trying to give him small feeds more often until he starts sucking and gaining weight. There's not much else we can do. He's a nice little fella and I wouldn't mind breeding from him later. Nick is interested in using him too. He wants to put new blood into his stock in the next couple of years and this guy isn't one of Nero's."

"Nero?"

Mum answered my question. "Nero is Nick's prized bull; your father has used him over our herd. He throws nice calves with good natures which isn't surprising considering Nero is a big pussycat. He's a real Houdini though and keeps getting onto our property to graze. He uses the bridge over the river that your dad and Nick constructed down where you plan to build. It saves the men having to travel to a bridge five kilometres up the road."

"Doesn't he get to your girls, dad?"

"No, he just comes over the bridge and grazes where the grass is greener at the side of the river. Nick is doing everything he can to keep the bugger in, short of tying him up which I wouldn't be happy about. He's in the middle of constructing an electric fence around the paddock and it should be finished in the next couple of days. If that doesn't keep Nero in, I don't know what will."

"I don't understand, didn't you say yours and Nick's cattle mingle and eat each other's grain? How come Nero isn't with them?"

"Fortunately, he hasn't had the sense to head in the other direction – yet. Once he does, he'll get to the girls and could become a problem."

Dad grabbed a notepad and pencil from beside him, moving them to where I could see. He drew a picture of both properties, divided by the river which acted as a boundary and used his pencil to explain.

"See the river here?"

"It looks a fair way from the house."

"About two kilometres away. There's a causeway there and in the dry, the river is very low. In drought, it reduces to a trickle. The cattle can cross back and forth quite easily when they are in the back paddocks. Where you are building here..." Dad pointed out the section on the map which was in the other direction from the house. "When Nero gets loose, he makes a beeline for the bridge to cross onto our property. I don't graze the herd in that western corner and so far he hasn't wandered up to the paddocks where I do."

"He sounds like quite a character."

"Mum and I think he is, Nick is ready to strangle him."

Dad marked an x where our home was and a y where Nick's was. He tore the sheet of paper away from the pad and handed it to me. I folded it up and poked it into the pocket of my cut off jean shorts.

"After I help with the calves, I'll wander down and take a look. I can start working out where my house and the other buildings should go."

"Make sure you wear a pair of boots, there are snakes around here and I don't want you wandering around in sandals or thongs. Take your phone with you, there's good reception out here. Call me or your father if anything happens."

I patted mum's hand, she'd always been a worrier.

"I'll be fine, mum. If I can look after myself in foreign cities, I'm sure I can take care of myself out here."

After coffee and helping mum to clear up the dishes, I changed into a pair of hiking boots, pulled my hair into a ponytail, grabbed sunglasses, a hat and headed outside to the barn where the calves were.

***

The door to the barn was open and I saw a young man seated on a stool inside. He was wrestling with a black and white calf who was determined to suck the giant bottle from the man's hands. When I entered, they both turned to look at me.

"Hi, you must be Emmalynne. Your dad said you'd be over. I'm Mick."

Mick attempted to do the gentlemanly thing and stand, but his loss of concentration and the sudden wrenching of the bottle by the calf knocked him off balance and he ended up on his backside. The bottle hit the floor and the calf protested noisily, joining in the symphony of mooing coming from the far end of the barn where the other calves remained penned away.

Mick retrieved the bottle, shoved the teat into the calf's mouth, effectively silencing it and plopped himself back on the stool.

I took a moment to look over the young man. I estimated he was in his early twenties as dad said he'd been seventeen when he'd first turned up in search of a job and my father had agreed to give him a go. Both Mick and Rusty, who'd shown up a few weeks later, had proven themselves to be hard workers and reliable during the five years they'd worked at the property.

Both men lived in a bunkhouse which I probably wouldn't see the inside of. It was their home and I would never infringe on their privacy. Dad had explained the two men usually let loose in town once a week when the following day was time off. Although my father knew they usually ended up with a skin full of alcohol, they'd never caused trouble or driven when drunk. They usually spent the night with friends and drove home the following day.

Mick was a tall man, a good six inches taller than my five feet ten inches and well-muscled. His dark hair was a mass of unruly curls, flattened in places thanks to wearing a hat. His eyes were amber, almost yellow in colour and he had a very cute smile.

"Would you like me to take over feeding her while you start on the next one?"

"Yeah, if you don't mind." I moved closer, Mick handed the bottle to me and stood.

I took his place on the stool while he strode to the other end of the barn. I was surprised with how strong the sucking motion of the calf was, I needed both hands to keep hold of the bottle as it hungrily guzzled.

When Mick returned, he had the tiniest calf I'd ever seen, not that I'd seen many. He was jet black and not much bigger than a dog. I was bothered by how quiet and listless he seemed and understood why dad was so worried.

I sat for a few moments watching as Mick attempted to cajole the little fella to latch onto the teat and suck. No matter what he tried, the calf showed no interest in drinking.

Meanwhile, the calf I'd been feeding was finished and headed straight for the bottle in Mick's hands.

I laughed and grabbed the recalcitrant baby around the neck, holding her back.

"What will I do with her?"

Mick held out the bottle. "Take this and see if you can get him to take it. I'll take her to the outside pen so she's out of the way."

We swapped calves, but instead of sitting on the stool, I sat cross-legged on the ground, placed the bottle off to one side and pulled the baby into my arms. He nuzzled the side of my neck with his soft nose, such a sweetie. Then, I got an idea.

"Listen, little dude. My dad is worried about you so how about you and I come to an agreement? I'll take you outside for a run around and then you have to drink everything in your bottle. We want you to grow into a big, handsome boy. The girls will fall in love with you and want to have your babies. So, what do you think?"

Who would have thought I'd be seated on a floor covered in straw, talking to a baby bull like I expected him to answer?

"I know you're supposed to stay inside, but I reckon sunshine and fresh air is just what you need. Come on, let's break you out of this joint."

I stood, found a slip lead on a peg on the wall and placed it around the calf's neck. After picking up the bottle, I led the little guy outside and into the sun.

I had no idea where I could take him, so we walked around to the back of the barn where I found a gate leading into a small, empty paddock. The calf now had a definite spring in his step.

We entered the paddock, closed the gate and I slipped the lead from around his neck. He peered up me before taking off at a clumsy run. I laughed when he kicked his hind legs into the air over and over before running in circles.

After a few moments, I whistled, his head jerked up and he came running back to where I sat on the ground.

"Have your bottle for me now."

I held the bottle towards him and he latched onto the teat. In no time at all, the milk was gone, a white ring around his mouth was the only remaining sign of it. He released with a loud pop when there was no more to be had. I hugged his neck, gave him a light tap on the rump, told him to go and play and he bounded off to the other side of the paddock. I watched as he sniffed at some of the plants before running again.

"Well, look at that. It appears we have ourselves a calf whisperer, Chris."

I jumped and spun around when I heard Greg speak. Dad, Greg, Mick and I guess it was Rusty, hung over the fence. I stood and moved closer.

"Emmalynne, meet Rusty."

"Pleased to meet you, Emmalynne."

I shook hands with a man who looked to be around the same age as Mick. He was around the same height and build but with brown hair and green eyes. They were both good looking men and I had a feeling they probably broke a few hearts in town.

"You too, Rusty." I turned to face dad. "He was depressed, dad. I don't blame him, being cooped up in a barn all day. He needs sunshine and fresh air."

"We always keep our sickly babies inside to protect them, never though it could make them sad, but looking at him now, I think you might be right, sweetheart. How about we put you in charge of looking after him, he seems to like you? I saw how he looked up at you after you hugged him."

I felt my face heat with embarrassment and wondered what the men must have thought about me talking about animals feeling sad.

"I'd like that, dad."

The other men agreed, I'd been smart to consider that the little calf might have been feeling down. None of them dismissed it as a foolish city girl idea. It made me feel good about myself and I realised, maybe I had a real affinity for poorly animals and what I had planned would make a big difference.

"He's all yours, sweetheart. That's the first full bottle he's had since he was born six days ago and I certainly haven't seen him so frisky. He'll still need to be fed at least twice during the night."

"I don't mind, I'll have to do it when I have the sanctuary. What if I feed at ten, two and six during the night and early morning?"

"That sounds like a good routine. We'll see how his weight goes and should be able to cut them out in a couple of weeks."

"Okay."

"Come on men, we have work to do. The cattle won't get themselves to the sale yards." Dad leaned forward and kissed my cheek. "Proud of you, sweetheart."

I watched as they sauntered off before sitting back down on the ground. I gave Brutus – yes, I'd already decided on a name, another half an hour or so to explore. When he trotted back over without being called and sat on the ground beside me, I knew he'd had enough.

I led him back to the barn and into the pen where Mick had laid out fresh straw. Brutus immediately flopped on the ground and within seconds, he was asleep. I stood and watched for a few moments before sensing Mick was behind me.

"He's good. You did great, Emmalynne."

"Brutus is such a cute little guy, he's fun to spend time with."

"Brutus?"

"His name."

Mick laughed. "Your dad said you'd give them all names."

"He deserves a name. I have a feeling the fights in him now."

"Thanks to you. The rest of the calves are fed and outside, will you be back down later?"

"Yes, I'll be here after lunch."

"I'll see you then."

Mick ambled away and I headed up to the house, there were a couple of things I needed to check out online.

CHAPTER FIVE

Once lunch was done and I'd helped clean up, I headed out to feed Brutus. No one was in the barn, but when I approached the pen he was kept in, a large brown and white border collie went on instant alert. His ears pricked and he jumped to his feet.

I held my hand out, palm down, he sniffed cautiously.

"Hi there, you must be Pilot. Are you watching over the little guy and keeping him company? You're a good boy."

At the mention of his name, the dog appeared to relax, wagged his tail and licked at the back of my hand. I scratched behind his ear which must have triggered a nerve in his leg and it began shaking violently. Brutus was now on his feet and watching us with interest.

"Hold on, Brutus, I need to find someone to help me organize a bottle for you."

I turned at the sound of someone entering the barn.

"Hi Rusty, could you show me how to get a bottle ready for Brutus please?"

"Brutus?" Rusty lifted an eyebrow in question.

"I named him."

The man glanced over my shoulder and into the pen. He grinned. "It suits him and yeah, sure I'll show you how to make up his bottle."

Rusty talked me through heating a mixture of colostrum and warm water in a microwave on a nearby bench. He explained that property owners kept the colostrum on hand in either powdered or frozen form. It was vital orphaned calves received it for the first few days of their life to help prevent disease and illness.

"He'll probably stay on this mix for a few days longer because he's been slow to develop. One of us will let you know when he can go onto a different formula."

"Okay."

The mixture was poured into a large white plastic bottle which Rusty removed from a cabinet. He then took a teat from a bucket and explained they were kept in a sterilizing solution just like a human baby's teat. Rusty attached it to the bottle and handed it to me.

"Thank you. Do you need help with feeding the others?"

"No, it's all good. That lot devour their bottles and they're only fed twice a day now. They're on pellets and calf meal. I only came down because Mick said he hadn't shown you how to do a bottle and we knew Brutus was due one. As soon as he improves, we'll get him on solids too and the milk can be cut back. Taking care of him is a huge help to us especially at the moment with having to get the cattle ready for the sales."

"Well, if you do need help with anything, please ask."

"Thanks."

I placed the bottle down on a bench, grabbed a lead, crossed to the pen and was thrilled when my little black calf trotted over. He earned a pat behind his ears for his enthusiasm.

"Come on, Little Bit, let's give you a run."

I opened the gate, slipped on the lead, grabbed the bottle and led him outside to the paddock we'd used earlier. Dad had agreed to leave it empty so we could use it. Pilot loped alongside beside us.

When I removed the lead from Brutus and released him, he stood for a moment, head slightly to one side as if studying me.

I waved my arm in the air. "Go on."

Pilot seemed to know what to do. He pushed his head into the side of the calf and gave a playful bark. Seconds later, the pair shot off across the dry grass.

It warmed my heart to watch them running and playing like excited children. I sat on the hard ground and watched for a while before whistling. Pilot raced back to me, Brutus hot on his heels.

Like earlier in the day, the calf accepted the bottle, the contents disappeared within minutes and the pair raced off again.

I waited patiently until the calf had decided he'd had enough and slowly ambled back. He settled on one side of me, Pilot on the other. I patted them both while gazing out over the scenery. Even though it was obvious drought had taken hold, it still held a beauty of its own.

I felt relaxed, content, knowing I was where I was meant to be.

***

I batted away a persistent fly as I wandered towards what was now my patch of land. The heat had intensified and I was pleased I'd thrown a long sleeve shirt on over the tank top I wore.

Bush turkeys scampered out of my way. Black cockatoos circled overhead in the cloudless blue sky. Off in the distance, I could see water dancing on the shimmer of heat.

To the right of where I stood, not far away, was a wide, sturdy looking wooden bridge. A patch of yellow flowers caught my eye as they waved in the slight breeze. I had no idea what they were, but they were pretty and to flower in what was an extremely dry landscape, they were certainly resilient.

I was on *my* patch of land now and stopped to peruse the area.

A thunderous noise pierced the previous quiet and I spun to my left to see a huge gray and white bull headed straight for me. He was closing the distance between us much too fast for my liking. I stayed where I was, hoping he would swerve and not barrel straight through me.

I guessed it was Nero, *the big pussycat* as mum had called him. He didn't appear to be slowing as he cleared the bridge and continued straight for me. City girl here – I had no idea what I should do. So, I held up one hand and shouted, "Whoa," as loud as I could.

He tossed his head and backed off on the speed. By the time he was close enough to touch, he had slowed to a walk and stopped.

I reached up and patted him. "You must be Nero."

The huge bull snorted and I reached out to scratch behind his ears. He obviously liked it because he began leaning into my touch, ensuring I continued.

"Like that, huh?"

When the sound of an engine echoed from the distance, I peered around the bull to see a quad bike headed my way.

It came to a stop nearby and holy hell, the man who stepped off it was the epitome of tall, dark and sexy. Very, very sexy.

He stomped towards us, an angry expression on his handsome face.

"God damn it, Nero. That's it, I'm sending you to the fucking sale yards. Someone can make dog meat out of you for all I care. I'm sick and tired of having to chase after you."

I stepped around the side of the poor animal who was being threatened with being turned into dog meat.

I held out my hand. "Hi, I'm Emmalynne."

The man appeared startled but shook my hand before quickly releasing it again. "Sorry, didn't see you there."

"I gathered." I scratched at Nero's chest and kissed his soft nose. "It's okay, baby. I won't let him send you to the dog meat factory. You just heard I was here and came to say hello, didn't you?"

"Are you kidding me? Who kisses a damn bull on the nose? A bull they don't know. He could have killed you. I mean he wouldn't, he's a big softy, but you didn't know that."

"I did actually. Mum and dad told me about him, probably so I wouldn't be scared if he got out and came over while I was here checking out my land. I knew it was Nero, he's the only bull around here except for dad's new bull calf who is very cute."

"How is the little fella? Chris was worried sick about leaving him to go down to Sydney for a few days. Has he had Laura out to take a look at him?"

"Not that I'm aware of. Brutus is doing very well now, he was only sad about being locked up in the barn all the time."

The man burst into laughter which I found irritated me. "You called him Brutus? Sad? Really? Next, you'll be telling me Nero escapes because he's lonely. I didn't know Chris had a hippy type daughter."

Ooh, this man was making me angry, an emotion I didn't succumb to very often. I slammed my hands on my hips.

"In case you weren't aware, I have read studies about animals and they get sad and lonely just like humans."

He laughed again. "Whatever you say, darlin', but I can guarantee you, Nero is neither sad nor lonely."

The way he sneered darlin' at me, raised my ire further. "How would you know?"

"I've been in this business for a lot of years and I've never once heard mention of a sad or lonely farm animal. Come on Nero, let's get your arse back home."

Nero grunted but turned to the man who slipped a lead rope through the ring in the bull's nose.

"I'll come back for the quad, you can keep it company in case it gets lonely while I'm gone."

He laughed as he led the bull towards the bridge which led to his property on the other side of the river.

"Very funny, you arrogant prick." I shouted after him.

He threw his head back and roared with laughter. I fisted the hands on my hips and eyed the quad bike. I was tempted to push the damn thing into the river but had been raised better than to do damage to a perfectly good piece of expensive machinery.

I had no idea who the arrogant arsehole was, but I hoped I didn't encounter him again.

***

NICK

So, that was Emmalynne Peters. The woman was drop dead gorgeous. Dressed in short shorts, her long legs seemed to go on forever. I could easily picture them wrapped around me as I drove into her. I started to become uncomfortably hard and reached down to adjust myself in the tight jeans.

As I led Nero back, I continued recalling the woman's features. Her long, very dark hair was tied back in a ponytail but some hung over her shoulder and fell below her breast. Speaking of which, why the hell hadn't she been wearing a bra? Her white tank top did nothing to conceal the large rosy peaks hiding beneath.

Blue eyes as clear as the purest sapphire had sparked fire when she'd become angry. I hadn't set out to upset her, but really, animals felt sad and lonely? What a load of crap.

"And you, Nero, what was that all about, sucking up to her? I get that you're friendly and like people, but you acted like you were in damn love when she was patting you. I must admit, I wouldn't mind her scratching me behind the ears. Or, somewhere else."

I led my pain in the arse bull across the bridge, up the hill past the house and into the horse stables. He wasn't a fan of being locked up, but it seemed acceptable if one of the horses were there. At least he hadn't attempted to kick his way out like he had when I'd locked him in the barn. Not yet anyway.

Both Cleo and Napoleon were stabled, so I pushed the big lug into a stable beside the mare. She hung her head over the door, took one look at him and snorted. It was as if she was disgusted that he was there. He snorted back in reply – I imagined he was telling her to suck it up.

Fuck, now I was imagining animals talking to each other thanks to the discussion with Emmalynne.

I grabbed a bucket and filled it with a good helping of grain.

"You really are a pain in my arse, Nero. I swear if you weren't in so much demand for your services, you'd be dog meat tomorrow."

Nero glared at me as if he knew exactly what I was saying, farted and took a large dump. All over the freshly spread straw.

"Fuck, Nero!"

I pulled the nuisance out and pushed him into the next empty stall, the last thing I needed was him rolling in shit.

I shoved the feed bucket in, even though I was inclined to let the bugger starve. Trouble was, doing that, would bring about carnage from the monstrous animal. I grabbed the wheelbarrow and cleaned the stall out for the second time that day. Jeff, Lonnie or Gaz would have done it if I'd asked, but I was already in a foul mood thanks to the damn bull and a gorgeous woman who I suspected was about to become the bane of my life.

CHAPTER SIX

EMMALYNNE

I stood watching, fuming, as the man led Nero away. I had to admit, the view of his arse encased in tight jeans was mouth-watering, just like the rest of the sexy man. Pity he had to be such a jerk.

I crossed to where he'd left the quad bike and noticed the keys had been left in the ignition. The temptation to drive it into the river was strong, but I could never be so heartless and bitchy.

It had looked like fun as he'd ridden towards me, bouncing over the terrain. Did I dare try? Or, should I wait and borrow one of dad's? This time the devil on my shoulder threw out a challenge I couldn't refuse.

I threw my leg over the seat and wriggled my butt until I was comfortable. When I turned the key, nothing happened. Checking the dashboard, I noted a button which read – 'start.' When I pushed it, the engine roared to life and the bike rumbled beneath me. I checked out the rest of the controls, it didn't look too hard to operate.

I shifted the bike into gear and pushed down on the accelerator. The black beast surged forward much faster than I anticipated. I hit the brake hard, the bike jerked to a stop and I was flung over the top and off to one side. I skidded along the ground on my stomach for what seemed like forever. The ground tore at the skin on my hands and shredded the skin on my legs.

When I eventually came to a stop, I burst into tears. The pain was excruciating. I didn't want to move and after lying still for a few moments, I realised I could no longer hear the beastly machine. With a great deal of effort, I pulled myself into a sitting position. In time to see Mr Sexy storming towards me.

The possessed bike was off in the distance, the angry man was headed from its direction. I assumed he'd manage to catch up with it and shut it down. The killer bike now sat waiting for its next unsuspecting victim.

Mr Sexy loomed over me. "What the fuck did you think you were doing? You could have killed yourself."

A fresh round of tears erupted and I swiped at the snot now oozing from my nose.

"Hell, honey, don't cry." He crouched before me, gently wiped my face with a handkerchief before holding it over my nose so I could blow.

"I'm sorry, it looked like fun when you rode it. I was angry at you, but I wouldn't put it in the river. I'm not that nasty. I'm so sorry," I blubbered.

"Honey, I have no idea what you're talking about. It is fun, but you need to know how to operate it.

He wrapped his huge work roughened hands around my wrists and turned my palms upward. Pieces of skin had been ground off, pieces of gravel had embedded themselves in the wounds and blood oozed everywhere.

He lowered them onto my lap. "You might...um....want to button your shirt."

I followed the line of his gaze and found my tank top was badly torn up and one of my bared breasts was on full display. Heat suffused my face as I pulled the shirt across my chest. The shirt was filthy but undamaged.

Tears erupted again when I found my injured fingers were too painful to use on such tiny buttons.

"Let me do it." His voice was soft and gentle, I found myself warming to him.

"Thank you." I peered up and my eyes locked with his dark gray, almost black ones for a few seconds.

Mr Sexy broke from the gaze and shook his head slightly before dropping his attention to my legs.

I looked down at the same time. "Oh my." Skin had been torn free, some had been rolled back and was hanging loose. Both legs also oozed blood.

"These need attention, honey. How did you get here?"

"I walked."

"Well, I doubt you can walk back. How's the pain?"

"It's more numb than painful now."

"Shock probably. I can take you back on the bike if you wouldn't mind."

"Yes, please, if it's no trouble."

The man stood, clamped his arms around my waist and hefted me onto my feet. The numbness I mentioned? Gone. The pain had returned with a vengeance. I stumbled against his hard chest, he wrapped his arms around me and held me close so I didn't fall.

"Whoa there, are you okay?"

I nodded as more tears jumped into my eyes. "Pain." I managed to breathe out.

Seconds later, I was lifted into his arms and we headed for the quad bike. Although I was slender and not particularly heavy, he carried me as if I weighed no more than a feather.

When we reached the bike, he looked down at me. "Will you be okay on the back? I can carry you to my place and drive you back around."

"I'll be fine, it's only a short distance and I've already caused you enough trouble."

"Don't women always." Although the grumble was under his breath, I'd heard it and wondered what lay in his past.

He lowered me onto the seat and climbed on in front of me.

"You'll need to wrap your arms around me, so you don't aggravate the wounds on your hands."

I did as he asked and rested my head against his back. He smelled of leather and cattle with an underlying musky scent. I melted against him, feeling secure.

The bike growled to life and he turned it towards mum and dad's homestead. I watched the scenery as we passed by. He took it slow, which I appreciated, every slight bump caused excruciating pain all over my body.

As we approached the house, dad and Greg appeared from around the side and watched as we moved closer. Mr Sexy stopped the bike in front of them and switched off the motor.

"Nick, what's going on?" dad's voice was filled with concern.

So, this was Nick Johnson. I'd expected a much older man, someone around the same age as my father.

Nick climbed from the bike. I stayed where I was not knowing if I'd be able to stand. As he opened his mouth to explain, dad noticed my bare leg which was nearest to him.

"What the hell, Nick? Explain. Now!"

"Dad! It's not his fault. I decided to try out the bike and it threw me off."

My father rounded on Nick. I felt sorry for him, the way my dad jumped to conclusions and blamed the man for hurting his baby girl.

"I..."

I spoke up, cutting Nick off. "It wasn't Nick's fault, dad. He left the bike to walk Nero back over to his property. I saw the key in it and decided to try it out."

"Sorry, Chris." Nick apologized, for what I didn't know.

Dad clapped him on the back. "No, it's me who should apologize to you. I'm sorry I jumped down your throat. Looks like this gal of mine is gonna need to be watched." He turned his attention to me. "Can you walk?"

Tears overflowed again, what the hell was wrong with me? I'd never been such a cry baby before. Maybe it was shock as Nick had said.

I shook my head, I had no idea how to get inside but it wouldn't be by walking.

"I'll carry her inside, Chris. I don't think there are any major injuries, but I would recommend she gets checked out and has a tetanus injection. You never know what's in the ground. My chopper is in, but I don't think it's an emergency. Taking her into Longreach by car would be fine.

"Do you feel like anything's broken, Emmalynne?" Dad asked.

"No. I'm sore but I'm pretty sure nothing is broken."

"Wait a moment, I'll get your mother."

Dad strode to the front door, threw it open and shouted for mum before returning to stand near me.

Mum appeared, wiping her hands on a tea towel.

"What are you shouting about, Chris?"

"Emmalynne had an accident and she's hurt. She helped herself to Nick's quad bike when he wasn't around and without his permission. She was thrown off." Dad stared daggers at me.

Mum gave me the once over. "Anything broken, sweetheart?"

"I don't think so."

"Fool girl, what did you think you were doing, using someone else's property without permission?"

I felt like a child back in primary school, being chastised for pinching something from one of the other kids. I deserved it, but where had my over-protective mother gone? In the past she would have been all a dither if we even stubbed a toe. This calm woman in front of me was a stranger.

"We'd best get you into town and patched up." Mum looked closer at my leg and tutted.

"I'll take her if I can borrow the truck, Chris." Nick turned his attention to mum. "Someone will need to carry her in and out of the surgery and no offense, Willow, but I don't think you're capable of doing that." He again addressed dad. "I know you're busy getting the cattle ready, Chris, so I don't mind helping out."

"Yes, we are and we're running a little behind." Dad raised his eyebrows at mum, silently questioning what they should do.

"We'd appreciate your help, Nick and no offense taken." Mum smiled at Mr Sexy.

"I need to get cleaned up first before going into town," I insisted.

Nick placed his hand on my arm. "Trust me, honey, the last thing you want at the moment is water hitting those wounds."

"But..."

"Alex has seen much worse, no one will think anything of it. Come on." Nick swept me into his arms and carried me to where dad's truck was parked.

Greg opened the front passenger door, Nick gently sat me on the seat and strapped the seatbelt across me before heading for the driver's side.

Mum leaned in towards me. "I'll call Alex and let him know you're on your way in."

"I need my purse; the doctor won't see me without having the details of my Medicare card."

"I'll give the receptionist the details over the phone," mum assured me.

Nick climbed in beside me and started the engine. Dad closed the door and they all stood watching as we drove away.

***

Nick started along the dirt driveway, headed for the highway. A few minutes after we'd left the house, he reached into the breast pocket of his check shirt, pulled out his phone and handed it to me. I winced as the slight weight settled in my hand.

The unlock code is 463189, can you go into contacts, dial Jeff – he's my foreman, and put him on speaker please?

I nodded and did as he asked.

"Yo, Nick, what's up?"

"Jeff, I've gotta do a run into town. Chris' daughter had a bit of an accident and I offered to take her in to see Alex. I'm not sure when I'll be back, but probably after dark. Cleo and Antony are rubbed down and stabled. Nero broke out again so I've locked him in the stables with some feed. When you bed Samson and Delilah down for the night, can you leave Nero with another bucket of feed and plenty of hay?"

"Sure, you don't want him paddocked?"

"No, the fence will have to be fixed again and he'll be fine where he is – I hope."

"Okay, do you want Lonnie to load the feed ready for the morning?"

"Thanks, I don't fancy I'll want to do it when I get home and you know how impatient they all are first thing. Can one of you milk Helen and settle her in the barn. The jugs will be picked up by Barry at around four this afternoon. After Achilles and Hector are fed, they can both go in the barn with the new calves."

"Consider it done."

"Thanks. If I don't catch up with you tonight, we'll talk in the morning. We still have changes on the contract to sort out with Lance regarding Nero's sperm."

"Yeah, he expects to get it for near on nothing. You'll need to put your foot down."

"I know, it's just……"

"I know he's a friend and like a lot of others, he's doing it tough, but you have given him a better than fair price. You have your own arse to cover too."

"Thanks, *dad*. Talk later."

Jeff laughed. "I've been called worse. See ya."

The call disconnected and I handed the phone back to Nick, he tucked it away in his pocket.

"What's with the names?"

He gave me a sheepish glance. "I like ancient history."

"Fair enough, I rather like them. It's a change from Bessie, Fido or Spot."

Nick laughed. "It certainly is."

"I'm sorry to cause you so much trouble, Nick."

"It's what we do out here."

"What's that?"

"We help each other out. Your dad is busy with cattle, your mum couldn't have carried you, so it made sense for me to offer. I would have done it for anyone."

Why did I feel a pang of disappointment at his statement?

"Tell me about this sanctuary you have planned."

"Dad talked to you about it?"

"Yep, he mentioned you'd be building on the land near the bridge and explained you would be taking care of injured and orphaned wildlife."

"Not only wildlife, domestic animals also. I'm going to organize a chat with Laura, the vet, to discuss fostering abandoned and unwanted animals. I'll set up a service to find them a forever home."

Nick turned the truck onto the highway and headed north towards town.

"It sounds like you have it all figured out. Will you release the native animals back into the wild once they've recovered?"

"Hopefully, but it will depend on how old they are, if they have healed well enough to be able to take care of themselves and if they need ongoing medications. It's something I'll need to discuss with Laura."

"I think you two will get along very well."

"I hope so, I'd like to work with her to help the animals."

Nick nodded and glanced at me for a moment before returning his gaze to the road.

CHAPTER SEVEN

"I'm sorry about how I acted earlier, even if I didn't understand what you were saying, it doesn't mean I should have been rude."

"You made me pretty angry, I have to admit I was tempted to push your quad bike into the river. I wish I had now instead of attempting to ride it."

Nick laughed. "Once you're healed up, I'll give you a couple of lessons so you don't get hurt again. They're basic vehicles, but sensitive."

"You reckon? I kind of found that out for myself. I barely touched the accelerator and it shot off like a damn rocket."

"Sensitive, as I said."

A comfortable silence settled over us. When we came up on the city limits, I straightened in my seat.

"I've been looking forward to coming into town, but it could have been under better circumstances."

"I'll give you the five-cent tour for now. On your left, the building with the curved roof is the

Australian Stockman's Hall of Fame and Outback Heritage Centre."

"I've heard a lot about the place from mum and dad, it's one of the first places I want to visit."

"On the right is the Qantas Founders Museum as you can see by the planes. Visitors can tour the insides of the aircraft and even walk on the wings of the 747."

"I thought Qantas began in Winton?"

"It did although locals say Qantas was conceived in Cloncurry, born in Winton and grew up in Longreach."

"I guess that keeps them all happy. Have you done the wing walk?"

Nick stole another glance my way. "No, not yet, maybe we'll do it together?"

"I'd like that."

"Up ahead, you can see a water tank, it's a recognizable land mark. To your left again are trees and bushes which are natives of the area. A pathway weaves through it all, it's known as the Longreach Botanic Walk and stretches for two and a half kilometres. There are signs explaining all about the plants and the part they play in the environment."

"I'm liking this tour, it's definitely value for money."

Nick laughed as he guided the truck through a roundabout. The road ahead had numerous stores on both sides. Quaint early twentieth century buildings sat side by side with art deco structures. I couldn't wait to explore.

"Main Street?"

"Yep, it's nothing like any of the big cities you're used to, but we can get everything we need or want."

"I prefer it to the city."

Nick turned the truck into a street with a signpost which read *Eagle Street* and a moment later, he eased up to the front of a building which had 'Doctor's Surgery' painted on the awning above. He switched off the engine and pulled on the hand brake.

"Do you mind waiting here while I go and check that Alex is around?"

"Of course, there's no point in putting your back out by hefting my weight if you don't need to."

Nick studied me for a moment, searching my face......for what? "Back in a minute."

He climbed from the truck, closed the door and strode to the glass door of the building and pushed it open.

When he returned, he was accompanied by a short, balding man wearing a suit. He must have been melting in the heat. I opened the door when they moved closer.

"Hi." I held up my hand in greeting, being unable to shake with the stranger.

"Hi, Emmalynne. Your mum called to say you'd had an accident and were on your way here. I'm Alex."

"Pleased to meet you, I think."

Alex laughed before taking my wrists into his hands and checking my palms. He frowned and it became deeper when he leaned in and studied my legs.

"What do you reckon, Alex?" Nick asked.

Alex stood back but kept one hand on the truck door. "Well, young lady, it's the hospital for you, I'm afraid. You'll need sedation so your wounds can be cleaned and treated without causing you too much pain."

"Damn, you sure you can't do it?" I dreaded having to wait at the hospital for hours and I'd caused Nick enough inconvenience.

"I could, but I won't subject you to so much pain." Alex turned to Nick. "I'll call the hospital and speak with Garth Windsor, he's on duty over there this afternoon. He'll take good care of you. Bye for now."

Nick closed the door after Alex stepped back. They shook hands and Nick climbed back into the driver's seat.

"The hospital is just off the highway near the Qantas Museum, so it won't take long."

"Thanks, Nick. You can drop me there and leave if you like. I'm sorry to have caused you so much trouble."

"Not as much as some." Nick grumbled under his breath before turning left.

Something he didn't like had obviously happened in his past.

**

Nick drove up to a sprawling white painted building, immaculately kept gardens and lawn dressed the front. The structure had an art deco appearance – I knew as much about architecture as I did about plants, but I'd seen buildings of that era in cities overseas. Brown painted French doors were spaced at regular intervals on both the upper and ground levels. It was impressive and beautiful, but not a place I wanted to become familiar with.

Nick eased the truck around a circular driveway and up to the front entry. He shifted it into park, pulled on the hand brake and switched off the engine. He climbed out, closed the door and hurried around to my side. I opened my door and he leaned in.

"Put your arms around my neck and I'll pick you up."

I did as he asked and he lifted me carefully from the vehicle, his muscles bulged beneath the sleeves of his shirt. Turning, he pushed the door closed with his backside and strode towards the entrance.

"Do you know where to go?" I asked as we stepped inside.

Nick laughed. "Honey, anyone who's lived on a property around here is very familiar with this place."

"That's not good."

"It goes with the territory when you're on the land, sooner or later something will happen."

Nick followed the signs leading to the emergency department. Once we arrived in the waiting room, he eased me into a chair and approached a nurse at the counter. We spent the next five minutes filling in forms and Nick had not long handed them back when a nurse appeared with a wheelchair.

"Emmalynne Peters?" she asked while glancing around the room.

"Here." Nick stood.

"Oh, hi, Nick." She approached with the chair and Nick lifted me into it before stepping aside.

I was wheeled towards a doorway and saw Nick hesitate. Turning, I placed the back of my hand on his arm and the nurse stopped our progress.

"Is it okay if Nick comes in?"

"Of course."

"Thanks, Grace." Nick smiled at the nurse and I felt a slight pang of jealousy – ridiculous.

I had no idea if he minded being with me, but I didn't want to be alone. I breathed a sigh of relief when Nick placed a hand on my shoulder and squeezed reassuringly.

Grace pushed me into a cubicle with a bed and pulled the curtain across. Nick lifted me onto the bed – he seemed to be lifting me a hell of a lot. The nurse removed my boots and socks and I prayed my feet didn't smell.

"I'm Grace and I'll be the nurse helping Dr Windsor today." She smiled while introducing herself.

"Nice to meet you Grace." I smiled back.

While she checked my wounds, Nick moved to the head of the bed, so he was out of the way. He kept his hand on my shoulder which helped me stay relaxed.

Grace had a clipboard and began asking questions. I answered them all and she proceeded to check my temperature, blood pressure and pulse. She then flipped over to another form.

"When did you last eat?"

"About three hours ago."

"Hmm, it should be okay. Dr Windsor will be in shortly."

"What will he do?"

"He'll give you sedation, a light anaesthetic then we'll clean and dress your wounds. You'll also have a Tetanus injection."

"Stitches?"

"Dr Windsor will make that decision once he has the wounds clean."

"Emmalynne Peters?" A man of average height and wearing thick eye glasses stepped up to the bed.

Grace handed over the clipboard.

"I'm Garth Windsor. Alex Jenkins called and explained you'd beaten yourself up with help from a quad bike."

"Hi, Dr Windsor. I'd shake hands but......" I held my hands up, palms facing outward.

"Garth, and that's fine. I'll take a look and see what we need."

"Thank you."

He lifted my hands and examined them closely, he then checked the wounds on my legs before turning to Grace.

"I'd like a full wound set up, Td vaccine and peripheral IV."

"Yes, Dr Windsor." She hurried away and the doctor turned back to me.

"I'll insert an IV for sedation, it's a light anaesthetic. You won't feel anything. I prefer to keep oxygen on during the procedure, do you have any issues with wearing a mask?"

"I've never had one, haven't been to hospital before. I don't think it will be an issue though."

The doctor nodded. "Grace will assist me with washing out your wounds. When that's done, I'll have a better idea of whether or not you need stitches. Once they're clean, I'll apply some non-stick gauze and bandage everything."

He then read from a form which detailed the sedation and I was asked to sign, giving permission. I did as he asked although my signature was rather ordinary.

Grace returned, pushing a silver-coloured trolley with all kinds of paraphernalia on top. She pushed it close to the doctor who moved it to where both he and Grace would be able to reach it.

"You'll be in the waiting room, Nick?" The doctor opened various packets.

"Yes, I'll go and park the truck, grab a coffee and wait. How long will it take roughly?"

"An hour or so. I'll send Grace for you when we're done."

Nick squeezed my shoulder and I smiled up at him.

"I'll see you soon, Schumacher."

I laughed and watched as Nick crossed the room and disappeared through the curtain. Jeez he had a sexy arse.

"Okay, let's get started."

The doctor swabbed my forearm and inserted a fine needle. I watched as he connected the IV and hung a bag from a hook at the head of the bed. Holding a needle up to where I could see it, he explained it contained the sedation.

"You won't be aware of anything once it takes effect."

"Okay."

My head spun as he pushed the contents of the syringe into a cap on the tube of the IV.

Darkness descended.

**

"Welcome back" Nick stood with his hand on my arm and a concerned expression on his face. "Garth has stepped out for a few minutes, he shouldn't be long. After he speaks with you, I can take you home."

"Will you help me to sit up, please?"

"Of course."

Nick slid an arm behind my back, another beneath my legs and lifted me into a sitting position on the side of the bed. I wavered slightly, but seconds later I was fine. I lowered my eyes to see my hands and legs were now wrapped in white bandages.

The doctor pushed through the curtain and stepped up to me. "How are you feeling?"

"Really good."

"Pain?"

"Not too bad, nothing a couple of Panadol wouldn't take care of."

Grace entered with a wheelchair. On the seat was a large white paper bag and walking stick. She gathered them and handed them both over to Nick who placed them on the bed beside me.

The doctor rested a hand on the arm of the wheelchair as he spoke.

"Everything went well. Some of the skin was rolled back in large patches but it was superficial. I cut away the rolls so there is a better chance of healing. Some of the wounds were deeper but not enough for stitches. You might have a bit of scarring but in time it will fade."

He took a deep breath before continuing.

"The wounds have had antibiotic cream applied and are dressed with nonstick gauze under the bandages. Panadol for pain should be fine."

He pointed to the paper bag. "You have antibiotics which need to be taken twice a day for five days. You also have cream and extra bandages. Keep the bandages dry for forty-eight hours. After that, you can have short showers but no baths for ten days. Apply the cream twice a day and keep bandages on for five days. If there is any redness or any area becomes hot to the touch, see Alex immediately."

"I will, thank you."

"You're welcome. The walking stick will help you to get around for the next couple of days, please return it when you no longer need it. Take things easy, you'll be a little sore and stiff. I recommend you stay away from quad bikes for a while."

I laughed. "I think I'll have a few lessons before I tackle one again.'

"Good idea. Let's get you into the wheelchair and on your way home."

Grace pushed the chair close and Nick lifted me in before shaking hands with the doctor and collecting the package and stick.

We left the area together and said a final goodbye to the doctor before heading for the entrance. While Grace pushed the chair, Nick walked alongside me.

We'd reached the reception area in the front foyer, when we heard a female calling Nick's name. I watched as he visibly stiffened.

"Fuck." Nick raked fingers through his hair as a petite blonde headed woman hurried towards him.

She stood before us and we all came to a stop.

"Maddie." Nick sounded pissed.

"Can we talk?"

"No, we've said all we're gonna say. I'm done, please leave me alone."

Tears welled in the woman's eyes but I had the feeling they were fake, for show only.

"Please, Nick. I made a mistake."

"You sure did. Now if you don't mind, I need to get this lady home."

The woman gave me a glare that could have set me on fire, talk about instant hatred. I was curious as to who she was and what was going on here.

"Nick, please, I need you."

"I'm sure Frank is capable of meeting your needs."

"It's over. It was a mistake, Nick. One time only," she whined.

"Maddie, enough. Leave me the fuck alone."

Nick strode off, Grace and I followed, we found him waiting outside. He led us to where the truck was parked, placed the paper bag and stick into the back seat and opened the front passenger door. I was lifted onto the seat and he buckled me in. Before he closed the door, I thanked Grace for her care.

Nick climbed in behind the wheel and started the engine. We both remained silent until he turned onto the highway.

"I'm sorry about Maddie."

"Do you want to talk about it?"

"Not really."

"Okay." I was dying to know what had happened between them but didn't dare ask as Nick's expression was savage.

Quiet descended again and minutes later, I'd dozed off.

CHAPTER EIGHT

I jolted awake when Nick turned onto the bumpy dirt driveway, sat up straighter in the seat and pushed hair from my face.

My hands had been bandaged with the fingers together, but the thumbs were bandaged out on their own. It afforded me some semblance of grip and would enable me to do some things for myself.

I gazed at Nick who seemed to sense it and flicked his glance my way.

"Tired?"

"A little. I guess the sedation will take some time to wear off."

"I've been thinking, maybe I should explain the scene back at the hospital."

"You don't owe me an explanation, Nick. Am I curious to know what it was all about? Of course, I am. I'm nosy like that, but you never have to talk to me about anything which makes you uncomfortable."

"You're different to most people I've met."

"Is that good or bad?"

"Good, you don't seem to want anything from me."

Oh, Nick. I can think of something I'd very much like from you, it involves wrapping my hands around your bare arse. I shook the thought from my head, but when Nick glanced my way and gave me a lopsided grin, heat hotter than Hades crept over my face.

"Please, please tell me I didn't say that out loud."

Nick laughed. "It seems the sedation has disengaged your brain from your mouth."

"I'm so, so sorry. I don't normally say things like that, but in my defense, you do have one hell of a sexy arse. The rear view of you in jeans is mouth wateringly good."

"Well, thank you, but it wasn't exactly what I was talking about when I said you didn't seem to want anything from me."

"What did you mean?"

"I grew up on a property just south of Winton. My parents are still there. It was started by my great-great-great grandfather as a small fifty acre spread. Over the years, extra land has been purchased and it's now two hundred thousand acres. It sounds a lot but out here where it's so dry, you need a lot of land to sustain your herd. Dad runs both cattle and sheep."

"Is that unusual? I thought sheep and cattle men were supposed to not like each other."

"Yes, normally owners run one or the other, but my grandfather felt it was wise to diversify. When the market for cattle falls, the market for sheep usually remains steady and vice versa. It would be unusual for both to fall at the same time."

"Wise man."

"Very. He made good money and some excellent investments over the years. He was worth millions when he passed. We'd always known he was wealthy, but we had no idea of just how well off he was. Grandma had passed on a few years earlier, so when he died the property went to my parents. A large amount of money was left to my brother and I. Stuart and I became instant millionaires. He stayed on to help dad run the property, I bought my own."

"You have a brother? Older or younger?"

"Identical twin, Stuart is older by twenty minutes."

"Wow, there are two of you?"

"Don't say that like it's a bad thing," Nick laughed.

"Oh, I didn't mean it that way. It's just...."

"What?"

"You must know you're a pretty sexy specimen of male. I've met and worked with some exceptionally good looking men in the course of my career, but you have them all beat on looks and sensibility. It's amazing there are two of you."

"Careful, you'll give me an ego."

"I doubt it, you don't seem the type. I've only known you a few hours, but I would have to say despite misjudging you at first, I think you are humble, hard-working and considerate. I'm a good judge of character, had to be thanks to the industry I was in and the people I was around, it could be a toxic environment. I'll tell you about it, but not now. Now is about you."

"Right, I'd be interested to hear about your life in the big smoke and all those countries overseas. I like to think I have all of those qualities you mentioned but add gullible to the list."

"Really? You don't strike me as a man to be easily taken advantage of, who was it who hurt you?"

"Madeleine Harris, the biggest mistake of my life."

"Sounds serious."

"It was. I met Maddie at the Spring dance last year. She's a pretty woman as you saw. She was new to town, so I did the gentlemanly thing and introduced myself. We danced, talked and I found we got along pretty well. After the dance, we exchanged numbers. I contacted her and we had a few dates. I guess we'd been seeing each other for about four months, hadn't done anything except kiss and hug, but I wasn't about to push – she turned up on my doorstep crying. She'd been thrown out of her unit because she'd been unable to find work and was behind on the rent. Alarm bells rang in my mind, but being the fool I was, I ignored them and invited her to stay until she was back on her feet."

Nick took a deep breath before continuing.

"I don't flaunt my wealth, people assume I have money because I own my place and try to help others out wherever I can."

I nodded. "My dad said there was a lot of gossip about you being rich, but no one really knew if it was true and if it was, no one knew how you'd come upon money."

"Yeah, I've heard whispers but it's not anyone's business."

"I agree."

"Coming from out near Winton, I've been a bit of a mystery man. I'm not one of the locals who know everything about each other. I've never opened up about my private life before, but there are two reasons why I feel comfortable talking to you and I felt I should explain about what happened at the hospital."

"I've told you, there is no need for an explanation. What reasons?"

"For some strange reason, I mean I've known you for all of about eight hours, I sense I can trust you to keep anything I say to yourself. The other reason is, I believe, thanks to your modelling career, you are wealthy in your own right, so I can be confident my money means nothing to you."

"True on both accounts. I would never break your confidence and I have more money than I could spend in five lifetimes with the simple life I now intend to live."

"So, as I said, you don't want anything from me."

"Hmm, you're wrong. I would like your friendship."

"That is something I'm happy to give you."

"Thank you."

"Anyway, back to Maddie. She hadn't been with me for more than a week when she suddenly insisted on helping out by looking after the property accounts. Alarm bells went off with the force of an air raid warning. I told her no one looked after my accounts but me. She said I didn't trust her and we fought about it. Next thing I know, she grabbed her purse, got in her car and left. I didn't see or hear from her for the following two days. When I went into town, I heard she'd been cozying up to Frank Winters. He owns a large spread north of Longreach, is a widower and old enough to be her grandfather. When I heard that, I was done. I saw her at the bank later, told her to come and gather the rest of her things and get out of my life."

"I'm sorry."

"Don't be. Two weeks later I heard she'd moved in with Frank. Rumour was, shortly after they fought. I'm betting she was trying to get control of his money also, but Frank is no fool and would have said no. She either left or he kicked her out."

"Where did she go?"

"She turned up on my doorstep again, crying and saying she was sorry. How I was the love of her life and it had hurt when I wouldn't trust her."

"You obviously didn't take her back. How long ago did this happen?"

"About a month ago. Every time we run into each other, she begs to talk to me. I've told her a dozen or more times, I'm done. It seems she just isn't getting the message."

"Do you still love her?"

"That's the thing. I liked her a lot but I didn't love her. There was never any chance of us sharing a future. We never had sex, I never had the urge to be with her that way. We didn't share a bed and hadn't kissed or hugged for more than a week."

"So, you were really only friends?"

"For me, yeah."

"Thank you, Nick."

He pulled the truck to a stop in front of the house.

"You're welcome. As I said, it's what we do around here. I knew how busy your dad was and your mum wouldn't have been able to lift you – not that you weigh more than a feather."

"No, I meant thank you for trusting me enough to confide in me."

He nodded, climbed from the truck and by the time he'd reached my side, I'd somehow managed to extricate myself from the seatbelt and open the door.

He lifted me into his arms, his warm breath caressed the side of my face as he carried me up the steps and into the house.

***

Dawn had broken if light streaming through the gap in the curtains was any indication. I lay in bed feeling as helpless as a toddler.

The previous night, mum had washed all the dirt and blood from me, applied some of the cream I'd been given to minor scrapes on my chest and belly and helped me to dress in a pair of sleep shorts and a tank top. This morning I planned to ask her to tackle my thick mop of hair which felt encrusted with dust and dirt.

It had been a long time since I'd hung my head over the side of a bathtub for my mother to wash my hair. I'd been about eleven and had broken my wrist falling from a trampoline.

I'd managed to get to the ensuite to use the toilet when needed with the aid of the walking stick. I felt like the tin man from *The Wizard of Oz* – the bandages prevented me from properly flexing my knees, limiting them to only a few centimetres of movement.

Dragging myself from the bed, I inched my way to the ensuite to take care of my full bladder. On my way back to bed, a soft knock sounded at the door. I called out for mum to come in – I knew it would be her come to check on me and I wasn't wrong.

"Morning, sweetheart. How are you feeling?"

I plopped onto the side of my bed, afraid I might topple over.

"I'm good, no pain, but everywhere aches."

"Bound to for a couple of days, you took a hard fall. I thought you would want to stay in bed?"

"No, I'd like you to help me wash, dress and come down for breakfast. Later, I'd love for you to wash my hair."

"It's been a long time since I did that for you."

"I was just thinking the same thing."

"You don't need any Panadol?"

"No, the restrictiveness of the bandages bothers me more than anything else. I'm sure I'd be fine without them."

"They can come off for a while tomorrow afternoon when we have to change them, but didn't you say they had to stay on for five days?"

"That's what the doctor said, but mum, I'm on antibiotics and have antibiotic cream. The chance of infection is miniscule. I promise I'll wear gloves before touching anything and I'll wear yoga pants until the wounds are healed. I can't stay like this for any longer than tomorrow. I'll be lucky to last that long."

"Your body, your decision, but I know you must be uncomfortable. I think I have a pair of cotton gloves you can use. I'll look for them later. "First off, let's get you organized and ready for the day."

Mum hovered nearby as I did my tin man impression back to the ensuite. She sponged my face, arms, chest and tummy while I perched on the toilet lid. After applying cream to my chest and tummy, deodorant under my arms, she helped me into a pair of sweat pants and a tank top. Lace up denim sneakers were then slipped onto my feet. I felt much better, much fresher even though a shower would have been welcomed.

"Have you seen the hiking boots I wore yesterday, mum?"

"No, the last time I saw them was when you left for the hospital, they were on your feet."

"I wonder where they are? The last I remember was when the nurse removed them after Nick sat me on the bed at the hospital."

"Maybe Nick picked them up and forgot to bring them in from the car?"

"Hmm, they could be in dad's truck, I'll check when Nick brings it back later today." The thought of seeing him again caused a flutter in my belly.

"He'll probably drop it here after he's done the morning chores." Mum pulled my hair up into a ponytail and secured it with an elastic tie. "Nice man that Nick."

"Yes, he is. We started off on the wrong foot, but I think we could be friends now."

"Just friends?"

I turned to face mum who had an eyebrow raised.

"Just friends, Mum. Nick was hurt pretty badly by his last girlfriend, I doubt he'll dip his toes in that water for a very long time."

"Shame."

"Mum, don't you go interfering."

"Me? Interfere? Never."

I growled at her before I grabbed the walking stick. We left the ensuite, crossed the bedroom and headed down the hallway to the kitchen. I was beginning to get the hang of my tin man walk and could actually move at more than a snail's pace.

CHAPTER NINE

Mum and I slowly entered the kitchen and dad glanced up from reading the latest news on his iPad. He set it down on the table and watched while mum assisted me to sit at the table opposite him.

"Morning, love. How are you feeling?" Dad meant well as did everyone else, but I had a feeling I was going to become sick to death of people asking me the same thing.

"I'm good. How's Brutus?"

"Mick took him out to the paddock at about five last night, he ran around with Pilot and King for a while before running to Mick for his bottle. After he'd finished, the three animals frolicked for a while longer before Brutus came back and lay down beside Mick. Not long after he was put back in his pen he crashed. The dogs were fed and when Mick checked a while later, both Pilot and King were snuggled in asleep with the little fella. They were still that way when Rusty checked on them at ten. Brutus took all his bottle again with no trouble, curled up with the dogs and went back to sleep. He's just had another feed and is in his pen. If he keeps this up, we'll be able to cut back on his feeds and introduce pellets and chaff. You did great, love. I thought we were going to lose him for sure."

"Thanks, dad. He hasn't been out this morning?"

"No. I asked Greg to let the boys know that you would probably take him out, but I'd inform them if you weren't up to it."

"I'd like to spend some time with him. I miss the little guy."

"Just don't overdo it." Mum, ever the worrier, patted my bandaged hand.

***

I stood with my back leaning against the wooden fence, watched Brutus sniffing at trees and pulling at the few surviving shoots of grass. I'd decided not to sit as I usually did, it would be a struggle to get back on my feet again.

The rumble of an approaching engine broke through the sound of birds chirping and cattle lowing in the distance. I turned to see Nick approaching, returning dad's truck. I raised a hand to wave and Nick greeted me with a megawatt smile before parking the truck, climbing out and closing the door.

A strange feminine flutter passed through my body as he strode towards me, coming to a stop on the other side of the fence.

"Good morning, you're looking a bit better."

"I feel pretty good but will be glad to get rid of these bandages. At the moment I'm walking like I have a stick up my arse, I have next to no movement in my knees."

Nick erupted in laughter. "Thanks for the visual."

"I've been calling it my tin man walk."

He chuckled again before cocking his head towards where Brutus stood pulling leaves from the lower branch of a tree. "How's he doing?"

"Very well. He's been taking his feeds without any problems at all, even the overnight bottles were guzzled down. Dad is stoked. I think one of the guys are going to weigh all the calves this afternoon so we'll know better how he's doing after it's done."

"I'm pleased for both you and your father. He's a nice little fella and should grow into a solid bull. I'd certainly be keen to use him if he turns out anywhere near as good as I think he will."

Brutus stopped destroying the tree, looked over at us and came trotting over. Nick climbed the fence and dropped to his feet at the side of me. The calf nuzzled against his hand.

"He can probably smell Nero."

"How is Houdini?"

"We kept him in the stables last night because no one had a chance to fix the fence in his paddock. When I went to check on him this morning, he was still asleep. I swear he's the laziest chunk of dog meat I've ever encountered."

"Nick! Don't talk about him like that, if he hears you, he'll get a complex."

Nick stared at me as if I'd grown an extra head, I had to admit, I had sounded pretty stupid.

"Forget I said that."

Nick nodded. "I fed him and left him while I took care of the horses and fed Helen. When I'd finished and wanted to take him out, he wouldn't budge.

"Oh dear, I guess it's not easy to move a bull of his size if he doesn't want to be moved."

"Definitely not. I left the stall door open, figuring he'd only head down to your land if he took off and slipped a lead on Helen to take her to the paddock. As soon as we passed his stall and headed for the door, Nero started following. It made me think about what you said yesterday."

"What was that?"

"About him being lonely. The more I thought about it, the more it made sense. I wouldn't want to be alone day in and day out. So, I put the two of them into Helen's paddock and they trotted off together. I'll wait and see what happens as time goes on. I'll bring them both into the stables at night so Nero has her and the horses for company. If it works out, it should stop him from breaking out."

"My ideas aren't so ridiculous after all?"

"We'll see, but thanks for giving me something to consider."

"You're welcome."

"What are your plans for the rest of the day?" he asked

"I'll probably sit out on the verandah, read and do a few crossword puzzles on my iPad. Should be interesting using only my thumbs. I'll also take care of Brutus in between. There's not much I can do."

"True. I was wondering if next Saturday, you would allow me to take you to the Outback Hall of Fame. They have a nice little café where we could have lunch."

"Why, Mr Johnson, are you asking me on a date?"

"I guess I am. Honesty dictates that I should inform you, it may become necessary for me to consider you more than a friend. How do you feel about that?"

"I'd definitely have to say I am interested in seeing what develops over time. There's an unmistakable spark between us. So yeah, being honest, I would like to see where this goes."

"Well, I have chores to get back to. We'll talk again soon. Oh, your hiking boots are in the back seat, I forgot to take them in last night."

Nick leaned over and brushed his lips over mine before turning and striding in the direction of his property.

I raised a bandaged hand to my lips which seared from the contact between us. My eyes stayed glued to the rise and fall of his arse until he'd disappeared into the distance.

"We most certainly will see where this leads."

My attention was drawn back to Brutus when he nudged my thigh with his head.

"I get the message. Come on, we'll put you back in your pen."

I slipped the lead around the calf's neck and led him back to the barn. I couldn't wait for the next few days to pass so Nick and I could go out on our date.

***

Date Day

I dressed in a strapless powder blue sundress which was cinched in at the waist and flared out to finish just above my knees. White sandals were the choice for my feet. I'd anticipated we would be doing a lot of walking, so I wasn't so foolish as to wear heels. A pair of sapphire studs in my ears were complimented by a sapphire and silver bracelet.

My hair was pulled up into a ponytail. I'd quickly learned that wearing it down in the hot weather was not a good idea. A light dusting of makeup, swipe of lip gloss and I was ready.

I gathered my purse and phone from on top of the chest of drawers, checked myself in the mirror one final time and headed to the kitchen where mum was baking. She turned from where she stood at the sink when she'd heard me enter.

"You look lovely, sweetheart." Her gaze wandered over me. "You can barely see the scars on your legs already. Given time, no one would even suspect you'd been so banged up."

"They have healed well, probably due to the fact I was in good health."

113

"I agree. Nick's eyes are going to about fall out of his head when he sees you in a pretty dress. Every time he's visited you've had shorts or sweat pants on."

"I know, it's nice to dress up a little."

"What time will he be here?"

I glanced at the digital display on the microwave. "Ten minutes or so. The place opens at nine. We'll have a bit of time to have a look around before the show starts at eleven. We plan to have lunch at the café after the show finishes."

A knock sounded at the front door and I hurried through the house to open it.

"Nick, come on in."

I stepped back and as he passed, he placed a chaste kiss on my cheek. For more than a week he had found some excuse to come over and spend time with me while I healed.

We had talked about almost everything, held hands as we walked over my land and I explained where I wanted buildings to go. We'd hugged and he'd kissed the top of my head, my cheek or a quick brush of his lips over mine. I was frustrated as hell. The man epitomized the word gentleman, but I was done. If he wasn't going to make the first move, I was.

Before he could go any further inside, I grabbed his hand, pulled him outside and closed the door.

"Emma?"

Remember I said earlier I hated the name Emma? Well, hearing it on Nick's lips made it sound downright sexy.

"We have a problem, Nick."

He visibly paled. "We do?"

"Yes. I admire you for acting like a gentleman, but I'm beginning to wonder if you like me at all."

"I like you very much."

"Then treating me like a virgin queen back in the 1500s stops right now."

I pushed into his arms, wrapped my hands around his neck, tangling my fingers in his soft curls and drew his head down to where I could reach. I crushed my lips against his. He must have felt shocked by my actions and it took him a moment before he wrapped his arms around me and took control.

Wow, did he take control. His hands cupped my arse, pulling me closer into him. My nipples became hard and unrestrained by a bra, pushed against the thin material of my dress. I felt the beginnings of a very impressive erection pushing against my belly.

His tongue forced its way into my mouth. I sighed and melted against him. My tongue dueled for superiority without luck. It sure was fun trying though.

When he lifted his head, we were both breathing heavily and our eyes locked. A moment later, my senses returned.

"That's a whole lot better."

"Wow!"

"Why didn't you attempt to kiss me like that before now, Nick?"

"I wanted to, believe me. I wanted to take you home, throw you on the bed and fuck you until you didn't know which way was up."

"Then, why didn't you? Was I sending you the wrong signals? I sure as hell wanted you."

"Your father."

"Dad?"

"I respect your father a great deal and I didn't want to disrespect him, your mother, or more importantly, you, by moving too fast."

"I appreciate that, but there's slow and then there was us – stopped."

"I overdid the go slow, huh?"

"Just a little."

"Does this mean you want to take things a little further."

"No."

Nick's expression turned to anxiety. "See...."

I placed a finger to his lips. "I want to take things a lot further. Let's go in and say goodbye to mum, I'll tell her to expect me when she sees me."

Nick placed his hands to both sides of my face and kissed me again. It wasn't as deep as the previous kiss but oozed with promise.

He released me, gathered my hand and led me back inside.

Glancing over his shoulder, he winked. "You look gorgeous by the way."

"You're mighty handsome yourself." And he certainly was, dressed in stone washed jeans and blue polo shirt with polished boots on his feet.

I couldn't wait to get the hunk naked. The muscles of my pussy clenched with excitement.

CHAPTER TEN

We headed along a road leading to a building with an interesting, rounded roof. It was quite inventive and different in design. Nick drove past a large statue which stood off to one side, turned into the carpark, pulled into an empty space and turned off the motor. By the time I'd removed my seatbelt and opened the door, Nick was in front of me offering his hand to help me down. Once on the ground, he closed the door and a loud beep sounded as the door locks engaged.

Nick kept hold of my hand and guided me towards the enormous statue.

"Ready for Nick's History 101?"

I laughed and nodded.

We stopped in front of the statue, I craned my head back and gazed up.

"It's huge! It didn't look so big when we drove past the other week."

"Yep, it's pretty impressive up close."

"Who is he?"

Nick pointed to a plaque on a sandstone rock. "A Ringer."

"A who?"

"A Ringer is a stockman who usually works with cattle. They're a vital member of any station or property. The statue is bronze on sandstone."

"Who made the decision to build the centre?"

"A man called Hugh Sawrey, a painter and stockman himself. Longreach had an historical role as a stock route junction and he wanted to honor it. He put up the initial funding and rallied supporters. There was a competition for architects to submit designs and Feiko Bouman, an architect from Sydney had his chosen. Queen Elizabeth 11 opened it in 1988."

"My goodness, Nick, you're a human history book."

Nick laughed as he encouraged me to stand in front of the statue, moved backwards, pulled out his phone and snapped a couple of pictures.

"Come over here so we can get the entire statue in and I'll take a couple of selfies."

When I joined him, he wound an arm around my waist, we both smiled at the phone and pictures were taken.

"Okay, let's go inside."

Nick clutched my hand, I studied the building and gardens as we approached the front steps. Two more selfies with the building in the background and Nick tucked the phone away in his pocket. Again, he wound his arm around my waist, setting my body on fire.

Once inside, my eyes were given time to adjust to the dimmer lighting after being in the bright sunlight outside, while Nick paid for our entry tickets and the show. With tickets in hand, he gathered my hand and directed my attention to one of the displays.

Above, hanging from an impressive curved ceiling of wood and glass hung a small aircraft with twin propellers. I was mesmerized as I gazed up at it. My first thought was how the hell had they gotten it in there?

"It's a retired Royal Flying Doctor Service plane which was recovered from a paddock in Mareeba near Cairns. Once out of service, it had been discarded and left to rust which was a shame. It was taken down to Brisbane by an aircraft restoration group I think it was, restored and brought back here in pieces. They assembled it inside and then hung it from the ceiling. Quite a feat."

"It was indeed. I was wondering how the hell they got it inside."

On the far wall behind the plane was an iconic Australian scene. A bright orange sunset illuminated two stockmen in front of a burning campfire.

From there we explored the museum which depicted the evolution of the Australian outback. The Aborigines who had lived on this harsh land 40,000 years earlier. Land baked dry by endless summers and washed away by savage floods, burnt by raging fires. The fact they still existed was a testament to their resilience.

Men and women from our pioneering days were suitably honoured – from the first Europeans who ventured to the area to stock workers, miners, saddlers, a teacher and others who helped to make the community what it was today.

The history of the Royal Flying Doctor Service from inception to present day was highlighted including a setup of a patient's treatment bed and equipment inside a plane.

A large polished wooden wagon had me fascinated. The words – Dava Singh General Merchant were painted in gold on the sides. It contained bric-a-brac, homewares and garments.

"What's the story behind this, Nick?"

"It was owned by a Sikh from the Punjab. He was a Hawker – travelling merchant. He would have visited the properties and stations to sell his goods. I suppose it would have been a valuable service for those who couldn't leave their homes very often to travel to town. Back then, some were a week or more away by wagon or on horseback."

The museum was a wealth of information of our past and I soaked it up like a sponge. There was another old wagon, memorabilia from R.M. Williams, a well know Australian man who had grown from swagman bushman to millionaire entrepreneur, old stirrups and beautifully tooled saddles.

"See these?" Nick pointed to gold medallions. "They were won in shearing competitions by a Ringer called Jackie Howe back in the late 1800s. He used shears which were more like a pair of scissors and sheared an incredible number of sheep in a matter of hours. His record wasn't beaten until 1950 but that was with machine shears. As far as I know, Howe's record with hand shears is still unbeaten."

"Wow! Why was he called a Ringer if he was a shearer?"

"It's the name they gave to the top shearer in the shed, pretty confusing really. We really do have incredible men and women pioneers."

It was almost time for the show, so we made our way back outdoors through a side door of the building, climbed a grandstand and took a seat. We looked down over a sandy arena below us.

Nick wrapped his arm around me and held me close. Butterflies were going crazy in my belly at the intimate contact.

"I didn't realise how little I knew about the outback. People were certainly determined and different. I don't know if I could have survived in such a tough landscape one hundred years ago."

"They were unique and as tough as the country they lived in. It's interesting to delve into our outback history. We learn about world cities and history while at school, but we're taught next to nothing about our own country."

"I agree. Then, once we're old enough, we want to flit off around the world, not realizing we have so much to discover right here in Australia."

Nick nodded in agreement. "I think it's why there is such a wide divide between country folk and city folk even these days. In the city, people demand everything at their fingertips and for the most part it is. They couldn't imagine having to go without because you've had a bad season or having to wait until the next truck comes to town.

People from both places work hard, but we really are worlds apart."

"It seems slower, more laid back out here," I mused.

"Don't be fooled. Country people are under enormous stress. Where those in the city have stress over deadlines and meeting expectations, we have enormous stress concerning weather which we have zero control over. Rain, or lack of it out here can make or break many a man or woman."

"Why do you do it, Nick?"

Before he could answer, the show began and our attention shifted to focus on a young man who introduced himself.

I loved the show he put on for us. There was a horse with a cheeky sense of humour, the ever-faithful dog and a small herd of sheep which were rounded up and penned. It was entertaining and had me laughing at times, gasping at others. The man was a working property owner who talked about life on the land. He was informative and talented. It was a performance I wouldn't forget in a hurry.

Nick assisted me down from the grandstand and we made our way back inside to the small café. We chose a table inside away from the scorching heat and seated ourselves.

I chose a chicken and mayonnaise sandwich with a side of fries and flat white coffee. Nick settled on a steak sandwich, fries and cappuccino.

Once the order was delivered, we settled in to eat and chat further. After swallowing a mouthful of sandwich, I asked the question Nick hadn't been able to answer before the show.

"As I asked earlier, Nick, why do you live out here? Why are you content to struggle with Mother nature year in and year out?"

Nick wiped his mouth with a napkin. "It's in my blood, I guess. I couldn't imagine doing anything else. Jeff has been studying, and started implementing, companion and sustainable planting for pastures with a focus on rotation. We've been trialing it on land which has been mostly unusable up until now. For the first time since I've been here, we have grass about a foot high and it's green even in this drought. Your dad is also giving it a go and is finding it successful. Most of the other property owners have scoffed at our ideas, but we have a few coming out next week to take a look. It should change their minds when they see the difference."

"Hopefully they'll take note of your success and try if for themselves. I imagine it would help relieve some of the stress during dry times."

"Exactly, it could make a world of difference."

We continued chatting about various aspects of the outback life while we ate and then drank our coffee.

Nick was an intelligent, knowledgeable man and it didn't surprise me to learn he had a degree in farm management as well as one in history. The man impressed me more with each passing day.

***

After taking a further look around the museum, we headed for the shop where I bought myself an *Akubra* hat. It would be much better suited to the conditions than the baseball cap I'd been wearing.

We left the building a little after two o'clock and headed for the truck.

"I'd love to come back for the dinner and evening show one day." I plopped the hat on my head when we stepped into the sunshine.

"I hear it's pretty good, the indoor arena is used for that show. I'll bring you back when you decide you would like to come. Where to now? Home or would you like to take a look around town? Most of the businesses will be closed but we can window shop."

"I'd love that if you don't mind."

"Of course not, Jeff, Lonnie and Gaz are taking care of things for me today, there's no hurry for me to get home."

"Town it is then." I grinned when he pretended to groan.

When we reached the truck, Nick held the door open while I climbed in. It was nice to be on the receiving end of good old-fashioned manners and when he slid behind the wheel, I told him as much.

The sun had been beating down relentlessly and the inside of the truck was like an oven. Nick put the air conditioner on full and blasted us with cool air as we drove the short distance to town. I noticed dark clouds above and drew Nick's attention to them.

"Do you think we'll get rain?" I asked.

Nick peered upwards for a moment before returning his attention to the road ahead. "They look to have rain in them, but nothing was forecast. We can only hope."

He parked the truck on Eagle Street and after helping me down, we held hands and strolled down the street.

I peered into the windows of several stores, one or two caught my eye and would warrant a second visit.

When we came across an arcade, I couldn't resist the urge to take a look. One store was named *Spinifex Collections* and through the window I could see all manner of unique objects and trinkets. Another discovery was the *Western Emporium*, a store created by local artisans. Women's clothing, handbags, soaps and locally produced crafts could be seen through the window. I definitely needed to be let loose inside.

We turned back into Eagle street and continued further on until we came upon *The Station Shop*. It was equally as intriguing as the previous two with objects ranging from leatherware to homewares, handcrafted souvenirs, books and toys.

I was certain the stores would hold a few pieces which I would love for my new home.

"It's a pity they're closed, but I suppose there will be plenty of time for me to come into town and take a look through. I need to come in on Monday to submit the plans for my house and the sanctuary buildings, so I'll ask mum if she'd like to come with me. We can do a bit of shopping and have lunch."

"Sounds like a good idea. I'm sure your mum would love to have a day out with you."

"It's been a long time."

On the other side if the street as we headed back to the truck, I came across a huge building with the name Kinnon & Co. Outback Outfitters & Heritage Gallery painted across the front. There was also a tearoom café and they organized tours in the area.

"This was once a Cobb & Co. Coach stop," Nick informed.

It was also closed and I placed it on my mental agenda for Monday.

"I'll have to check out their clothes. Since I'm going to live here, I'll need to look the part."

Nick laughed as we crossed the road back to the truck. "You have a hat, that's a good start."

I laughed and agreed with him. Once we had settled back in the vehicle, Nick turned to face me.

"Have dinner with me at my place. I cook a mean spag bol and garlic bread."

"I'd love to but I'm not sure I want to breathe garlic breath all over you when we kiss."

"We're going to kiss?" Nick grinned.

"Plan on that and more."

"A lady who knows what she wants and doesn't mind saying so, I like that. I better make it herb bread then. The last thing I want is to breathe garlic all over you."

"It's a deal then, take me to your abode, sir."

"Consider your wish, my command."

He turned back in his seat, flashed up the motor and we headed out of town.

The butterflies were back, excitement at the thought of being completely alone and intimate with the man I was beginning to care about.

CHAPTER ELEVEN

Nick drove around a bend on his driveway, his twenty-two-kilometre driveway, and a house atop a grassy hilltop came into view. The sun was setting behind it and the home was framed by bright pink, yellow, red and orange colours. It was stunning.

"Your place?" No, it wasn't a stupid question, out in these parts it could have been the home of one of his stockmen.

"Yep."

After negotiating the rise, he pulled the truck to a stop in front of a colonial log home. Two blue heelers raced up to greet us as Nick helped me down from the truck.

Nick pointed to the dog on the left. "This is Hector and the other mutt is Achilles. They're working dogs but they usually live in the house with me unless we have calves. I know they shouldn't, they're not supposed to be treated as pets, but......." He shrugged.

I laughed and patted the dogs who were busy sniffing and licking at my hands. When they'd had enough and run off, I straightened.

"This is gorgeous, Nick."

"Thanks. I designed and built it with the help of tradespeople from town. Mum decorated and furnished it."

The home was impressive, built from rough hewn half logs with polished wooden French doors at regular intervals opening onto a wide verandah which was supported by thick wooden beams. The doors stood wide open and Nick explained, when others at the back were opened, they allowed for natural air flow throughout and helped to keep the inside cooler.

Unlike my parent's home, the verandah disappeared along both sides. Mum and dad had only one at the front, another across the back.

"Your verandah wraps right around?" We stepped up the front steps and headed for the front door.

"Yes. I've always loved the colonial style and it keeps a lot of sun and weather off the logs which will help give them a longer life."

"Good idea."

Nick opened the front door which was polished wood with a shiny brass handle and lock, similar to those on the French doors.

When we stepped inside, it was noticeably cooler, proof the verandahs did keep the heat at bay.

The natural wood theme was carried through to the interior, heritage wood furniture was complimented by dark brown sofas dotted with bright yellow cushions. A book case overflowing with books was pushed into a corner, it was obvious where Nick got his knowledge from. A television was mounted to the wall above a unit which housed various pieces of electronic entertainment.

The living room, dining and kitchen were housed in one enormous area. A hallway off the living area led to what I assumed were the bedrooms.

Like mum and dad's home, it was single level. The kitchen had shaker style cupboards, stainless steel appliances and white granite bench tops. The floors were a light coloured slate.

Nick crossed to the fridge. "Beer or soft drink?"

"Soft drink please, any kind."

He grabbed a beer for himself and poured lemon soft drink into a glass before he handed it to me.

"Come on out the back." Nick indicated the door off the kitchen.

He stood back and allowed me to step through first. I swear my jaw hit the wooden deck beneath my feet.

Nick burst into laughter. "That's the reaction I usually get, not that many people have been here. Welcome to my oasis."

Oasis, indeed. Off the back deck was a beautiful, lush garden and lawn. Frangipani trees around the perimeter were bursting with flowers in pink, yellow and white. Acacias reached towards the sky. Jade and other succulents were a riot of colours. The small lawn would have made many people I knew in the city as jealous as hell, there wasn't a weed in sight. And in the centre of it all, was a sparkling pool with a waterfall of rock decorating one end.

"I have no words, Nick."

He guided me to a lounge chair and held my glass while I seated myself. After handing it back, he settled into one beside me. As I sipped at my drink, I watched birds frolic from one tree to another, bees sucked nectar from flowers. It was a piece of lush paradise surrounded by the harshness of dry land.

Hector and Achilles joined us, flopped down on the deck and rested their heads on their paws.

"How do you keep the pool full, doesn't evaporation affect it? I mean, it's not as if there is an abundance of water out here." People struggled to water their cattle so how could Nick maintain a pool?

"The other side of the paddock is a spring fed dam, I top it up from there."

"That's fortunate."

Nick nodded. "I don't make it common knowledge, otherwise I'd have people traipsing all over my land. If someone was in desperate trouble, I'd organize for water to be delivered."

"Do many people have pools?" There would certainly be a use for them in the baking heat.

"A few but not many, as you said, water is too hard to come by."

***

"I've been meaning to ask you a question but kept getting sidetracked. So, tell me why you left the exciting world of modelling and travel to come and live out here?"

"I was never really meant to be in the world of modelling. The travel was exciting at first, but after a while I was sick to death of planes and living out of a suitcase. When mum called to say her and dad had finally made the decision to move and had sold the house in the city to come out here, I was as jealous as hell."

"Why haven't you been out to visit?"

"Blame mum and her sneakiness. Whenever I was in Sydney, her and dad insisted on coming down to see me. I stayed with Craig and Marley and mum insisted it was good opportunity for them all to catch up with me. In reality, she knew if I came out here to visit, I would quit modelling straight away. She worried it would push me into making a premature decision."

"So, you waited until you'd had enough and your career had run its course?"

"In some ways, but the death of my best friend in a car accident a few months ago was the catalyst. I realised I didn't want to be away from my family anymore, so when the contracts expired, I refused to renew. I didn't need the money thanks to what I'd earned and investments dad had made for me."

Nick gazed at me thoughtfully. "It was time for you to follow your dream."

"Yes, it was. I knew I wanted to settle in the outback, having mum and dad already here was perfect. I've been happier here in the past couple of weeks than I have in the previous ten years."

"Maybe you lived your previous life in the outback?"

Nicks comment surprised me, he didn't seem to be the kind of person who would believe in multiple lives.

"I don't know but I feel drawn to the land. I honestly believe this is where I was always meant to be." I sat up and turned towards Nick. "Maybe I feel that way because I'm destined to be with you."

***

"Yo, boss! You around?"

"Out the back, Jeff," Nick shouted back before he stood, offered his hand and helped me to my feet.

A man around the same age as Nick stepped onto the back deck and approached us. His hat was held in his hands. I gave him the quick once over. He wasn't as tall as Nick but appeared to be as well-muscled with dirty blonde hair, chiseled jaw and blue eyes.

"Oh, sorry, I didn't know you had company." Jeff smiled my way.

"It's okay, Jeff. Meet Emmalynne, Chris and Willow's daughter we've been hearing about."

Jeff held his hand towards me, but before I could shake with him, he drew it back, wiped it vigorously on his jeans and thrust it back out. I shook hands and he held on a little longer than Nick liked if the scowl on his face was any indication.

"Jeff is my foreman and best friend from school, but if he holds onto your hand like that again, he could find himself out of a job."

I was shocked by Nick's words but when I glanced up at him, his eyes danced with humour and we all laughed.

"Everything is done. Nero and Helen are in stables next to each other and the big fella seems pretty happy. I think it's going to work out well putting them together. Nero didn't bother with the fences at all today."

"You can thank Emmalynne, it was her idea." Nick smiled towards me.

Jeff raised an eyebrow and Nick explained.

"Emma said Nero was getting out because he was lonely and looking for company. At first I thought it was a fool idea, but the more I thought about it, the more I realised she could be right."

Jeff bowed towards me. "Well thank you, ma'am. If we can keep the nuisance contained, it will save us all a hell of a lot of work."

"You're welcome," I said.

"Lonnie and Gaz are in town and I'm on my way to mum and dads for the evening. I'll catch up with you in the morning."

"Thanks, mate." Nick gathered my hand and I saw the two men exchange glances.

"Night, and thanks again Emmalynne."

***

I helped Nick with dinner by dicing tomatoes and chopping basil while he took care of the onions and garlic.

"Looks like we can't avoid garlic tonight." I indicated the press in Nick's hands, he was currently squeezing the life out of two cloves of garlic.

He stopped what he was doing and gave me a concerned look. "Should I leave it out?"

"No, you can't have spaghetti Bolognese without garlic, it wouldn't be the same. It doesn't bother me unless it bothers you."

"I'm fine with it, the sauce would be rather bland without it." Nick returned to squeezing the garlic and added it to the pan beside him which already contained the chopped onions and a dash of olive oil.

"Secret recipe?" I enquired.

"Nah, mum bought me a CWA recipe book and proceeded to teach me how to make a few things. She was convinced if I could at least cook a few dishes, I wouldn't starve to death. It's a long way to drive for takeaway. I've been trying out other recipes in the book and I'm getting rather good. It's usually enough for four so I normally freeze the leftovers and heat them in the microwave another time. Now and again, the guys and I get together for a barbie and swim." Nick stirred the sizzling ingredients in the pan.

"Do you cook?" he asked.

"A little. When I stayed with Craig and Marley, she would teach me some recipes. I didn't get to cook very often, I was either travelling or stuck in hotel rooms which didn't have facilities."

We continued putting our meal together and while Nick dished up the pasta and meat sauce, I took the herb bread from the oven and placed the slices onto a plate. Once everything was on the table, he crossed to the fridge.

"Beer, wine or soft drink?" He asked while holding the door open.

"I'll have a beer thanks, no need for a glass."

Nick placed a cold bottle in front of me and while he sat on the opposite side of the table, I screwed off the lid and took a swallow.

I watched as he curled pasta onto his fork before shoving it into his mouth. I did the same. The food was delicious with the right balance of spices.

Nick placed his fork down and took a gulp of beer before gazing at me thoughtfully.

"Ask me, Nick." I sensed there was something he wanted to ask but was hesitant about overstepping his boundaries.

"Why is there no boyfriend? I mean, you're gorgeous. Men should be falling all over themselves to be with you. Although I must say, I'm very pleased there isn't someone special."

I finished chewing the food in my mouth before answering. "There was a man – Josh. We were together for three years before we broke up two years ago. He hated the travelling involved in my career and the attention I received from other men. He wanted me at home – the outdated 'women should be barefoot and pregnant' attitude was strong in him. He was a good man in many ways and I wanted it to work, but his insecurities tore us apart and in the end, I was the one who walked away."

"No one since?"

"No. I decided it wasn't fair while I had so many demands on my time."

"I must admit, I would have been as jealous as hell, having other men ogling my girlfriend, but I don't believe you're the type of woman to betray a man."

I shook my head. "I'm not and never would be."

We finished our food and sipped at our beers. Nick's eyes sparked with desire as he continually looked me over.

"I want you, Emma." Nick spoke quietly but desire dripped from every word.

I pushed back my chair, stood and rounded the table. Nick moved his chair away from the table but stayed seated.

Lifting my dress, I straddled his thighs, scooted close and wrapped my hands around his neck.

CHAPTER TWELVE

I want you too, Nick." I lowered my head and crushed my lips against his.

Nick's hands slipped beneath my dress and cupped my arse in his palms. Our tongues pushed back and forth, fighting for control. I nipped his lower lip and he groaned before pushing the top of my dress down. My breasts bounced free.

Nick broke the kiss and gazed down at my milky white breasts, dusty pink nipples, pebbled and hard.

"Fuck, you're beautiful." He latched onto my nipples with his work roughened finger tips.

The lace of my panties offered no resistance to the denim of his jeans, I felt his hardened dick pushing to get free.

Feather soft kisses rained down over my face before my lips and mouth were taken hostage in an all out assault.

My fingers weaved through his silky soft hair. I wriggled on his lap, pushing against his hands, rubbing my pussy on his dick. I wanted, needed, so much more.

When he finally released my mouth, I was a trembling wreck.

"Nick."

"Bedroom. Now."

I wasn't about to argue and scrambled off him before stumbling down the hallway and through a doorway to our right.

The room we'd stepped into was huge, the furniture was wood, but it wasn't the time to spend taking in details. One glance at the large, king sized bed and I knew where I wanted to be.

Nick tossed back the covers before he rummaged in a drawer of the bedside table and recovered a condom. I took the opportunity to divest myself of clothing and shoes and freed my hair from the elastic tying it back.

When Nick turned around, I stood naked before him, my hair bounced over my shoulders as I stepped towards him.

His eyes burned with desire, he stood stock still, licking his lips and taking in every inch of my body. I didn't miss the movement in his jeans as his dick danced, protesting the restriction placed upon it.

Reaching out, I gripped his shirt and wrenched it free from the waistband of his pants. Nick took over, ripped it over his head and threw it aside. My fingertips caressed every contour of his magnificent chest. His physique would have put many male models to shame.

Fingers danced down my back and gripped my arse as we kissed. Nick's voice was raspy when he spoke.

"God, you're stunning Emma. I knew you would be. You really are a perfect example of beauty inside and out."

"Thank you, but one of us is wearing far too many clothes."

"I can fix that."

Nick kicked off his boots and the rest of his clothes disappeared onto the floor in a flash.

My eyes dropped to his groin. I didn't have a lot of experience to judge him by, but I certainly liked what I saw. He wasn't as long as I'd seen before but he had an impressive thickness which caused my pussy to clench.

He snagged the condom from the bedside table, ripped open the package and rolled it on. I gathered him in my hand and smiled at him when his dick flinched.

I was lifted into Nick's arms and placed on the bed before he crawled on and hovered above me.

"I'm going to enjoy exploring every inch of your delectable body, you'll be begging me to fuck you," Nick warned.

"Well, stop talking and start doing."

"Pushy little thing, aren't you?" Nick pushed my arms to the side.

Kisses rained down all over my face, along my collarbones and the sides of my neck. I squirmed with want. Arched my back, attempting to rub my pussy against the hardness of his cock.

A kiss to my lips and Nick worked his way down my body. He captured first one, then the other nipple. Sucking, nipping and blowing warm breath over the tortured areas.

My breathing was choppy, fingernails clawed his back before moving to grip his biceps which bulged with the effort of supporting his weight.

He sucked, licked and kissed his way down my body and finally focused his attention at my core which ached with want. He slid one finger inside me, I arched my back and humped against it.

"Nick, please."

"I know, honey, I can feel it."

Nick lowered his head and his tongue joined the finger inside me. My orgasm built and when the finger curled and hit on the sensitive bundle of nerves, I spiraled out of control.

My hips lifted from the bed and I pushed myself further onto the invading finger and tongue. Wave after wave of ecstasy crashed over me. Nick was relentless, refusing to stop until I was spent. He withdrew and gazed up at me, the evidence of my orgasm shone on his chin and around his mouth.

"Fucking gorgeous." He licked his lips before crawling back up my body – kissing, nipping. Until his lips met mine in a sensual kiss. I tasted myself on his tongue as it twisted and dueled with mine.

Positioning himself at my entrance, he slid inside, filling me completely.

"God that feels good, Nick."

I rocked against him, he pulled out and pushed back in. The walls of my pussy stretched to accommodate him. Muscles clenched as the familiar signs of an impending orgasm spread over me.

My hands were everywhere – in his hair, down his back, clutching at his spectacular arse. I ground against him, feeling him deeper with each thrust. When I felt his cock pulsating, I knew he was close.

I couldn't wait any longer, the orgasm crashed over me. My head spun, body trembled. I felt like I'd been hit with the force of a tsunami.

Nick growled, tightened his arms around me and I felt the warmth as he spilled into me, kept back by only the thickness of a single layer of latex.

***

I awoke in Nick's arms, one leg thrown over his thighs, my head resting on his chest. I felt happy and content.

When I wriggled to free myself from his grasp, he tightened his arms around me.

"Five more minutes." Nick's voice was hoarse with sleep.

"I need to go to the bathroom," I whispered.

"Damn, what time is it?"

Nick released me, I sat up and peered at the clock on the bedside table. "Five thirty."

He groaned. "Time I was up, I have work to do."

"Anything I can help with?" I leaned over and gazed at Nick's face, I could see he was fighting to wake up after our long night of making love.

Eventually, his eyes flickered open and he half smiled. God he was adorable with his mussed-up hair and sleep glazed eyes.

"Why are you so wide awake?" He grumbled.

"I'm used to sleepless nights and early mornings. Do you mind if I use your shower?" I bent forward and planted a kiss on his lips.

"Of course, I don't mind."

I scooted off the bed and padded to the ensuite.

"Nice arse," Nick called from the bed.

I gave it a shake and he laughed.

"Can I join you?" Nick stood in the doorway.

"I'd like that." I flicked on the tap in the walk-in shower. Water rained down on me from above.

Nick stepped in with me, wrapped his arms around my waist and kissed me senseless.

His hands wandered over my body before two thick fingers slid inside my pussy.

I latched onto his morning wood and with the aid of the water, my hand slid up and down. My thumb caressing the tip with every pass.

He groaned. I moaned. I was insatiable when it came to this man.

I found myself pushed up against a tiled wall, Nick cupped my arse and lifted me in his arms. I wrapped my legs around his hips and he slid deep inside.

One, two thrusts and he froze.

"Fuck." He sounded annoyed but I wasn't sure why.

"Nick, what's wrong?"

"Condom, or more precisely, lack of."

"Oh. I'm clean and on the pill."

"I'm clean too, do you mind not using one?"

"Not at all, I think I'd rather enjoy riding you bareback."

Nick laughed and crushed his lips against mine as we rode each other to the heavens above.

After washing and drying each other, we dressed and headed to the kitchen. While Nick fed the dogs and let them outside. I made toast and coffee.

We sat opposite each other at the table.

"What are your plans for today?" Nick asked as he munched on a piece of vegemite toast.

"I did offer to help you, but I think I should go home, change and see how Brutus is. After that, I have nothing. Why?"

"Yeah, the dress you're wearing is very nice but not very practical for working on a property. Do you ride?"

"No, I've never been on a horse in my life."

"Would you like me to teach you? Delilah is very gentle and we could ride down to my favourite spot in the river and have a swim."

"I'd like that, sooner or later I need to be able to ride. What time would you like me to come back?"

"Around two?"

"Perfect, anything I should bring?"

"No, I'll grab a couple of towels and drinks." Nick stood, gathered the dishes and packed them away in the dishwasher. I stored the toaster back in the cupboard and wiped down the bench tops.

We stepped outside to find the sky bruised with dark clouds and the parched ground showed the faintest signs of moisture.

"Looks like we got a spot of rain overnight but doesn't appear to have been much. I didn't even hear it on the roof."

"Well, you were distracted by other things."

"Indeed." Nick let out an ear-piercing whistle and I turned to watch Hector and Achilles racing towards us.

"Time for work, boys." Nick patted each of his dogs.

He gathered me in his arms and we shared a toe-curling kiss.

"Will you be okay to get home or would you like me to take you?"

"I'll be fine and you have work to get started." I gave him one last peck on the lips and started off down the steps.

"I'll see you around two," Nick called.

"On the dot," I called back.

***

Mum pounced the minute I entered the kitchen. "Hi there, did you enjoy your time with Nick?" She held up the coffee pot. "Coffee?"

"Yes, please." I dropped into a chair at the table.

Mum poured me a mug of coffee and one for herself before sitting beside me. As she sipped at the hot brew, she studied me.

"You look relaxed and happy."

"I am and yeah, I did enjoy spending time with Nick."

"Do I hear a but?" Mum lifted an eyebrow.

I shook my head. "No buts. I think Nick could be special. Do you know what I mean?"

"Your soulmate. *The one*." She patted my hand. "I knew you two would click."

"How did you know that?"

"Mother's intuition, I guess. From the first time I met Nick, I recognized the qualities I saw in him were what you complained were missing in Josh."

"When you and dad spoke about him, I assumed he was around your age. Why didn't you tell me he was only two years older than me?"

"I didn't mention his age because it didn't really come up in conversation. It's not my fault you made an assumption and thought he was much older."

I narrowed my eyes, searching her face. Mum had kept the information from me deliberately, of that I had no doubt. I just didn't know why she'd kept it from me.

"Do you think you have a future together?" Mum asked.

"I don't know yet. We've only known each other for a couple of weeks, I'm not ready to make predictions. I don't want to jinx things."

Mum stood and crossed to the sink, I followed. The mugs were washed up, I dried and they were then hung on hooks over the bench.

I'm going riding with Nick this afternoon."

Mum spun to face me. "Horse riding?"

"He's offered to teach me and we're going down to the river for a swim. It should be interesting."

Mum kissed my cheek and gathered her handbag from the bench top. "Be careful. I'll be gone all day, Carol Lintner and I are headed down to a station near Barcaldine. Alice Mortlock, one of the CWA regional members is ill. Will you be home tonight?"

Heat spread over my face and mum smiled.

"I see."

She started for the door but I called out. "Mum."

She stopped and turned back. "Yes?"

"I'm going into town tomorrow, I need to put the plans into the council. Yesterday afternoon, Nick and I took a stroll around town and there were a few stores I'd love to have a closer look at. I was hoping you'd come with me. We could have lunch while we're there."

"I'd love to. It's been a long time since we've had a girls' day out."

"I'll let you go and see you in the morning."

I kissed her cheek and headed for my room to change.

CHAPTER THIRTEEN

NICK

I saddled Samson and Delilah, led them outside and hooked their reins through a hitching rail which ran along the side of the stable wall.

When I glanced at my watch, I was surprised to find it was almost quarter past two. Emma hadn't seemed to be the type of person who would be tardy when expected.

I glanced in the direction of the bridge below, there was no sign of my lady. *My lady?* Since when had I begun thinking of her as mine?

"Jeff," I shouted.

He appeared from around the side of the stables.

"Yeah?"

"Have you seen Emmalynne?"

"No, should I have?"

"She said she'd be here at two on the dot. We planned on taking a ride down to the river and having a swim. I didn't think she was the type who would be late, or not turn up without calling."

"Lonnie and I were working on the fence Nero broke down the other day, we were there until a few minutes ago. We would have seen her cross the bridge."

I frowned and glanced back to the bridge. An ominous feeling grew in my stomach.

"Something's wrong."

"Don't jump to conclusions, Nick. You don't know if she's been held up by something."

"Trust me, she's in trouble."

I set off running down the hill, hoping I wasn't panicking for no reason. I heard Jeff's footsteps close behind, he caught up with me on the bridge and we ran side by side. The moment we crossed the river and stepped back onto the ground, I sighted Emmalynne. She was standing in the pasture doing a great impression of a statue.

"Emma!"

She didn't acknowledge my call, not even her head lifted. Her gaze remained firmly fixed on the ground in front of her.

"Fuck. Fuck. Fuck." Jeff grabbed my arm and his panicked voice had me pulling to a stop.

"What the fuck are you doing?" Panic was making me react angrily.

"Nick, calm down." He pointed towards Emma.

"What?"

"Snake."

"What the fuck?" I narrowed my eyes and stared in Emma's direction.

Sure enough, less than a metre from where she stood, a snake sat reared up. Alert and ready to attack. Bile rose in my throat. I couldn't see what type it was, but there were two deadly species which were common to this area – Eastern Brown and Red-Bellied Black. It could also have been one of the many harmless types which populated the area, but I had no way of knowing from where I stood and I wasn't about to take a chance with Emma's life.

"Nick, go to the left, grab a branch from one of the gums. I'll go to the right and try to draw its attention."

Jeff released my arm after giving instructions and as I moved to the left, he moved in an arc to the right.

My heart was beating a million miles a minute. Sweat beaded on my forehead and the palms of my hands turned sweaty. I snapped off a branch from the first tree I came to and crept closer to Emma.

"Stay still, honey," I whispered. "You're doing great."

She didn't move an inch, tears streamed over her face. I ached to take her in my arms and keep her safe, but I knew any sudden movement from one of us could get us bitten. We could then be faced with a life-threatening situation.

Centimetre by centimetre, Jeff and I moved closer. I was now close enough to see the snake was an Eastern Brown, the deadliest in our country. We were both a couple of metres from Emma when Jeff nodded his head towards me and stamped his foot.

The movement had the desired effect. It drew the snake's attention immediately and it turned away from Emma to rear up at this new threat.

I flew over the short distance, scooped the snake up with the branch and flung it off to one side.

Once clear of the danger, I dropped the branch and Emma threw herself into my arms, trembling and sobbing into my chest. I ran my hand over her back and kissed the top of her head. Relief flooded through me – she was safe.

"Sssh, its okay now," I soothed.

"I'll head back, Nick."

"Thanks, mate. I'll take Emma home and be back soon."

Emma lifted her head and gazed up at me through tear-soaked eyes.

"No, I'm okay. I want to go riding."

I peered down at her.

"Please, Nick, I'm fine. The snake surprised me and I wasn't sure what I should do. I knew you'd come for me.

"You did?"

Emma nodded her head. "I knew you would sense it wasn't like me to be late and come looking for me. You would know I was in trouble."

"He insisted you were in trouble," Jeff agreed.

"Gut feeling." I crushed her to me. I hadn't realised the depth of my feelings until I'd seen her life threatened.

Tilting her head back, I kissed her deeply, relief poured from us both.

"You scared the living daylights out of me. I'm beginning to think you should have come with a warning label." I gazed into her beautiful eyes and thanked God she hadn't been harmed.

Jeff groaned at our display of affection. "I'll leave you lovebirds to it. I have research to do on the computer for a couple of hours."

I turned and pulled Emma into my side. "We'll head back with you."

"Thank you both for helping this damsel in distress." Emma glanced up at me.

"Any time," Jeff answered. "But please don't make getting into trouble a habit."

"I'll always be here for you, honey." I planted a kiss to Emma's cheek before we started for where the horses were waiting.

***

EMMALYNNE

I clung onto Nick as if my life depended on him as we headed to his property. By the time we reached the horses, my trembling and rapid heartbeat had finally settled.

"Catch you later." Jeff lifted his arm in a farewell gesture before he disappeared around the side of a building.

"Are you sure you're okay?" Nick asked when we stopped where the horses stood waiting patiently. Their coats glistened in the sunlight. Both were jet black, one smaller than the other. The larger one snorted when Nick patted its rump. "This is Samson. You'll be on Delilah. She's the smaller, quieter, less opinionated one."

"I'm fine. I've been looking forward to riding all morning." The sky had cleared to a deep azure blue with only the occasional white fluffy cloud as added decoration. The sun shone brightly, not good for this drought-stricken town but perfect for swimming.

"Okay. Grab onto this." Nick indicated what I knew was the saddle horn.

I wasn't totally ignorant although I knew I had a hell of a lot to learn about outback life. I placed my right hand around it and held tight.

"Put your left foot in the stirrup and pull yourself up. Swing your right leg over Delilah's back to the other side."

In theory, it sounded simple and there shouldn't have been an issue. In practice, totally different story.

I positioned my left foot and bounced on my right to generate oomph to propel me upward. Somehow, I ended up being spun in a circle and crashed into Nick's very hard chest. His arms immediately took hold of me. I looked up into his face and dissolved into laughter.

"I'm guessing that wasn't how it was supposed to work?" I planted a quick kiss to his lips as he laughed.

"Not exactly, although I can't say I mind having you in my arms and pressed up against me. Take two?"

I nodded, turned back to face the horse, gripped the saddle horn, placed my left foot in the stirrup and bounced again to gather momentum. This time when my right foot left the ground, Nick's hands cupped my backside and I was pushed upwards. My right leg swung over the horse's back and I dropped firmly into the saddle. I fist bumped the air, elated with my success.

"Yes! Now what?"

Nick laughed, patted my knee, unthreaded the reins and placed them into my hands. He then explained the process of holding them loosely, pulling on the right one to go right, left one to go left and back on both to stop.

He adjusted the stirrups so I was more comfortable and asked me to keep my heels pressed down.

Once I was ready, I watched as he grabbed Samson's reins and effortlessly swung himself into the saddle. Yes, I did take a good long look at his sexy jean clad arse. I looked forward to having it filling my hands when we returned to the house later in the afternoon.

Samson started off and Delilah followed without me having to say or do anything. The two beautiful beasts ambled alongside each other as we crossed through the pastures. It was a wonderful experience, having such a strong animal beneath me.

"How does it feel?" Nick asked.

"Wonderful. I think I could come to love being on the back of a horse."

"I hope so, I love it. I ride for work but riding for pleasure is different – letting the horse run free beneath me. There's no other feeling like it."

"Can we run?"

Nick shook his head. "Not on your life. Not until you are more secure in the saddle. I care about you a great deal, but remember that warning label I mentioned? No, we'll stick with walking for now."

"Spoilsport." I pouted.

"A spoilsport who wants to keep you safe and in one piece." Nick pointed ahead. "The swimming spot in the river is just over the crest."

I nodded and we ambled towards our destination in silence.

***

As we crested the small hill, the meandering river came into sight. The water level was clearly down but it continued to flow.

The horses descended the other side and Nick brought Samson to a stop where the ground was flat and there was plenty of shade from huge river gum trees. Delilah followed suit without me having to pull back on the reins.

Nick dismounted and lifted me down. The animals wandered beneath one of the trees and began tasting the grass.

"Will they run off?" I asked Nick.

"No, they're good, they'll stay around here and be content to munch away on the grass. It's thicker here thanks to the river so they'll enjoy a good feed."

Nick headed for one of the saddlebags on Samson and pulled out two large, colourful towels and two bottles of water, he handed one over to me. I twisted the top off and drank thirstily before putting the cap back on and placing the bottle beside one of the towels he'd laid out.

The surrounds were peaceful –river gums and bushes of various types lined both sides of the riverbanks. An area in front of where we stood was open and there was a small, sandy beach. It was perfect – private, secluded with only the sounds of trickling water and birds chirping overhead.

"This is pretty, do you come here often?" I gazed up at Nick and wondered if he'd brought all the girls he'd known to this idyllic spot. For some reason I wasn't happy thinking he had been here with other women.

"I come here now and again." I noted the cheeky glint in his eyes. "I've always come alone before now, so you can turn down your jealousy meter."

"Oh." How the hell had he known what I was thinking?

"Did you wear a swimsuit, or are we swimming naked?" Nick wiggled his eyebrows up and down and I laughed.

"I have swimmers on."

"Damn," he grumbled.

"I think you'll like them." I unfastened the buttons on my shirt and pushed it from my shoulders, revealing a neon pink bikini top. The shirt floated from my fingertips to the ground.

Nick's eyes narrowed and he licked his lips.

I bent forward, removed my boots and socks before straightening again. My eyes were locked on his as I plucked the button of my jeans free and slid down the zipper, before spinning away from him. I kicked the jeans free before turning back.

Nick had a predatory smile on his face and he took a step towards me.

"Well, fuck me. I believe I like that view almost as much as the naked one."

I was dressed in a skimpy g-string which had my backside on full display. I'd worn it in a photo shoot and once I was done, I'd been told to keep it. The expression of sheer carnal hunger on Nick's face made me very pleased I had. It was one I would remember for a long time to come.

"Do you like it?" I held my arms out to the side and turned slowly around in a circle.

When I faced him again and dropped my eyes to his groin, there was no doubt about how he felt. His cock strained against the confinement of his jeans.

"I fucking love it!"

I stepped close, wrapped one hand behind his neck and drew his face down so I could kiss him. My other hand plucked open the button of his jeans, made short work of opening the zipper and slid inside his shorts. His dick was rock solid and when my thumb flicked across the crown, the liquid proof of his desire was evident.

Nick pushed me away and latched onto the arm inside his pants. When he attempted to pull my hand free, I latched on tighter. He growled, swept me into his arms, which forced me to release him and dropped to his knees on a towel before laying me down.

His eyes burnt with desperate need as he stood, stripped and dropped back down. His cock bounced against his belly, the evidence of his desire glistened in the sunlight.

Within seconds, I lay naked before him, the bikini tossed off to one side.

"Fuck, Emma." His gaze devoured me before his lips slammed against mine. I was taken in a relentless, breath stealing kiss.

I bent my legs, dropped my knees to the sides, opening myself to him. Silently begging him to take me.

His fingers invaded my pussy while his mouth and tongue savoured my nipples. Sweat beaded and we slid against each other. I arched into his touch, anxious for more. So much more.

"I can't wait any longer, honey. I need to be inside you." Nick positioned his cock at my opening and slammed home.

Yep, his cock was at home inside me, where it belonged.

Our fucking was frantic. Legs and arms tangled. Moans and groans filled the peaceful air around us. We were completely lost in each other.

I shattered first, my fingers clawed at Nick's sweat slicked back. I knew my nails would leave marks, but at that moment in time, neither of us cared.

Nick's cock pulsed within me, he let out a primal moan and his seed was emptied deep inside me.

When we both felt sated, he rolled onto his back, pulling me on top of him. He cupped my arse and stayed buried inside me.

I opened my eyes to find him staring at me, a strange expression on his face. He licked his lips, opened his mouth and closed it again.

"What did you want to say, Nick?"

He shook his head. His dick flinched inside me. "I'm falling for you, Emma. I don't know why, or how it's happened, but there's something about you which has gotten under my skin and captured my heart."

"Oh..."

"I know it's only been a couple of weeks and I keep telling myself I'm delusional – people don't fall for someone this fast, but I'm completely sane and I feel how I feel."

I remained silent, stunned by Nick's admission. No, it wasn't one of love, that would have scared the shit out of me. This was a genuine, heartfelt declaration that he cared about me and I was elated.

"Emma?"

I placed my fingers over his lips and gazed deep into his eyes – eyes full of hope.

"Nick, I have been around gorgeous men for all of my adult life. I've even thought I loved some of them, like Josh. But you're different. There's something about you which makes me feel like I'm only half a person when we're apart. I think about you every minute of the day and night. Do I love you? No, not yet, but I care very deeply for you and I think it's only a matter of time before that care grows into love. I think what we have between us is very special, I believe we were meant for each other."

He sighed deeply, seemingly content with my declaration, wrapped me in his arms and kissed me with so much feeling, I felt it deep in my heart. His dick surged back to life, hardened with me and I found myself desperate for him again.

Bending my knees, mindful to keep him inside, I pushed myself up and with both hands on his chest, I rode his dick.

The thickness inside me grew, the inner walls stretched to accommodate him. I linked my fingers behind my head, tilted my head back and bounced up and down.

Nick's rough fingertips squeezed hard at my breasts, pinched at my nipples. It was a mixture of pleasure and pain which rocketed straight to my core and had me coming apart.

He held my hips, his fingers dug into my soft skin. I was pulled down onto him while he thrust up. Moments later, he groaned my name and warmth filled me.

When he quieted, our breathing was ragged. I flopped forward onto his chest. Nick squeezed me tight and kissed the top of my head. I was exhausted and the happiest I had ever been.

I was falling hard for Nick Johnson. I only hoped he was ready to catch me.

CHAPTER FOURTEEN

Two Weeks Later

Brutus had greeted me like a long lost friend when I'd fed and taken him out earlier, even though I made a point of being with him at least twice every day.

Although he was now strong enough to be in the paddock with the other calves, he still seemed to be excited to spend time with me, Pilot and King in the small side pasture.

He was developing beautifully and raising him had taught me a great deal. Dad was over the moon and was already planning the calf's future.

After showering, I slipped into a pair of dress jeans, buttoned on a pink shirt – one I'd purchased at Western Emporium a couple of weeks before and pulled on a pair of western style cowgirl boots. My hair was swept up in a ponytail, lip gloss applied, silver hoops in my ears and a silver bracelet at my wrist. A spritz of *Chanel N° 5* and I was ready to go.

The previous night had been the first one in two weeks I hadn't stayed at Nick's. He'd driven up to Winton for the bachelor party of one of his friends and had spent the night with his parents and brother. I hadn't seen him since three in the afternoon, but we'd texted each other what seemed like a hundred times. I could only imagine what his friends had been saying if they knew. To say I'd missed him terribly was the understatement of the year.

I glanced at the clock on my dresser, it was almost half past nine. My man would arrive at any time.

I headed down the hall to the living room, before I could turn towards the kitchen, a knock sounded at the front door. I raced towards it, threw it open and flung myself into Nick's arms. He lifted me off my feet, I pressed my lips against his and kissed the ever-loving daylights out of him. When he set me back on the ground, I smiled up at him.

"I missed you," I confessed.

"So, I see. Maybe I should spend the night away more often if that kiss is an example of my welcome home."

"I promise you, it's only a taste of what I plan for later."

"Maybe we should just go to my place now?"

I hesitated, it wouldn't be a hardship to spend the morning in bed with him.

"No, I promised you a day out and it will make later all the sweeter. I missed you too. Are you ready to go? You look gorgeous as always."

"Thank you. I only need to grab my purse. Do you want to say hi to mum?"

"Yep, lead the way."

Grasping his hand, I led him through to the kitchen where mum was studying something in a book – most likely a recipe she wanted to try out on dad."

"Mum, Nick's here. We're going to get going."

Mum lifted her head and stepped closer, a smile on her face.

"Mrs Peters," Nick greeted.

"Nick. I suppose I'm never going to get you to call me Willow, am I?"

"It doesn't seem right. I don't mean to offend you, but mum and dad insisted on us calling our elders Mr or Mrs I guess it stuck."

"I understand darlin'." Mum turned to me. "You won't be home tonight?"

I glanced at Nick who gave me a cheeky grin and shook his head.

"No, but tell dad I'll see to Brutus as usual, in the morning and at lunch time while Nick does his chores."

"I will." Mum kissed Nick's cheek, then mine. "Have a good time and Nick, watch out for her on the wing of the plane. You know what she's like."

Nick wrapped his arm around my waist. "I won't let anything happen to her, you have my word."

"Jeez, anyone would think I was clumsy. I've had what......four or five mishaps?"

"Seven!" Mum and Nick spoke in unison before laughing.

I pouted in protest but knew they were probably right. "See you tomorrow, mum."

"Enjoy yourself and I expect to hear all about it tomorrow."

***

Nick eased the truck into a space at the Qantas Founders Museum car park and stepped out. By the time I'd unfastened the seatbelt, he had my door open and helped me down to the ground.

He gathered my hand and while he locked the vehicle, I stared up at the huge 747 aircraft.

"Does the tour guide take you out on the wing of that plane?"

"Yep, they sure do."

"It's a long way off the ground, isn't it? I didn't realise how big those planes are."

"You know you don't have to do it, don't you?"

"Yeah, I might have to give it some thought."

Nick kissed me before we headed for the entrance. The now mandatory selfies were taken in front of the building before we made our way inside.

In the interior gallery, stunning displays were everywhere, covering the history and evolution of Qantas over the past almost one hundred years

Nick paid our entry and while we waited the few minutes for our tour to commence, we checked out a few of the displays.

It wasn't long before the tour guide approached us and introduced herself as Hannah. We were the only two on the tour so we would have her undivided attention.

She led us through the displays, giving the history as it unfolded. I was fascinated and enjoyed hearing the history of three planes which had been a part of the first Qantas fleet. The museum had full scale replicas of all three. The first of these was a de Havilland DH-61 Giant Moth – I was amused by the name. The aircraft was a large, single-engine bi-plane, built in the 1920s in England for use in Australia as passenger planes. They carried six – eight passengers and were the first aircraft with toilets. They were taken out of service in 1935 because the engines were unreliable.

The next plane we heard about was a de Havilland DH-50, also a single engine bi-plane built in the 1920s as a transport aircraft. One had been converted to an air ambulance in Longreach, renamed – *Victory* and used by the Royal Flying Doctor Service to service the inland missions. It was their first aircraft; the year was 1928.

The one which really captured my attention was an Avro 504k Dyak. It was a two seat aircraft which had been developed to be a WW1 bomber bi-plane. *Qantas* had used one of these on a scheduled airmail service between Charleville and Cloncurry. The service had commenced in November 1922 and was the first scheduled air service in Australia. The initial contract had been for twelve months.

"I reckon the pilot needed a bloody medal for flying that thing. It looks so flimsy," I said.

Nick nodded in agreement. "They would have flown in all weather too. Better them than me."

We followed Hannah outside to where she explained there was a Boeing 747, 707, DC-3 and Catalina Flying Boat. The others looked so small against the huge 747.

We climbed the stairs of the narrow, sleek, 707 and stepped into the cabin. Hannah explained this was the world's first practical jet airliner and Qantas had been the fifth company in the world to place an order for them. The first had been handed over in 1959 and was aptly called – The City of Canberra.

Services to the USA had commenced in July of the same year. The cabin was narrow with two seats on each side of the aisle. They were much larger than the seats economy passengers were expected to squeeze into these days. There was a galley at the front and a smaller one at the rear.

Hannah led us to the cockpit and encouraged us to take a seat in the pilots' chairs.

"Can you imagine having to learn what all these buttons and leavers are for? I'd never be able to remember which did what?" I pushed on a lever which looked like a gear stick and was informed it was a joystick which allowed the pilots to alter the rise or fall of the aircraft.

I glanced over at Nick who was studying the dashboard.

"Trying to figure out how to fly it, Nick?" I joked.

"I was just thinking, I've seen the inside of cockpits on television and in movies but being in one is a little surreal. I have to admit, I'd struggle to remember what everything is for."

Hannah laughed. "Wait until you see the 747. You'll understand why pilots undergo so much training although a lot is computer controlled these days." She explained a few more interesting details before she led us out of the aircraft and towards the 747.

This was a plane I was much more familiar with as far as the seating and facilities were concerned. Hannah led us to the cockpit and we again sat in the leather seats. We'd thought the first aircraft was a maze of buttons and levers, but it had nothing on this one. It boggled the mind.

Hannah pointed out various functions and once done, Nick had a good look around the interior. He'd never been on an international plane before, having flown only in Australia.

Our guide directed us to a side escape door which led onto the wing. One peek through the space for me was enough, I decided to pass on the wing walk. It was a hell of a long way off the ground and I was terrified of heights.

After Nick was fitted with a harness and given safety instructions, I excused myself and headed back outside.

While Nick performed a few one legged poses with his arms in the air, I'd snapped a few pictures before he disappeared back inside. A short while later the two of them joined me back on the ground.

The next plane became my absolute favourite – a 1944 Catalina Flying Boat. The one on display had been purchased in Spain where it had been used as a water bomber. The flying boat had a special significance to Australia as Qantas pilots had flown them to keep supply lines open between England and Australia, breaking the blockade over the Indian Ocean when Singapore fell to the Japanese in WW11. The aircraft was a recent addition and an interactive display involving the plane was in the process of being planned.

We'd been at the museum for a little over three hours when my stomach grumbled loudly, reducing us all to laughter.

"I think lunch must be next on the agenda," Nick declared. He slipped an arm around my waist and we followed Hannah back inside, thanked her for the informative tour and headed for the restaurant. We took a seat and opened the menus.

Headings such as – Early Take Off, In-Flight Bites, Excess Baggage, Maximum Payload and Junior Flyers had me laughing out loud and Nick was also amused.

Beneath the headings were selections such as 707 Beef Burger, Nancy Bird Burger, Avro Rib Fillet Sandwich and Hudson Fysh of the Day.

I selected an unimpressively named Caesar Salad with chicken and a soft drink. Nick chose the Avro Rib Fillet Sandwich and also elected to have a soft drink.

The food was delicious and while we ate, we discussed what we'd seen and how knowledgeable Hannah had been.

It had been a fabulous day and soon it was about to get even better.

CHAPTER FIFTEEN

After leaving the museum, Nick surprised me by not heading towards home. He turned onto the highway and headed north out of town.

"Where are we going?" I was curious as to where we were going.

"I want to show you something," Nick answered cryptically.

"What?"

"Wait and see, Miss Impatience."

A short distance from town, he turned off the highway and we followed a road which led into the bush.

He came to a stop at the river and we climbed from the truck. He rounded the vehicle to join me.

"Where are we?"

"This is Longreach Waterhole, otherwise known as *The Waterhole*."

I held his hand as I looked around. There was a large picnic area with barbeques and the tables were covered with shelters. Some couples were enjoying an afternoon meal, we nodded in greeting and they called out hello.

About twenty metres away was what Nick said was a popular camping area which also catered to big rigs. A disused bridge across the river was in a state of disrepair but added to the character of the surroundings. Although the river was down due to drought, it continued to flow and there was an abundance of bird life.

The huge river wound for what seemed like miles in both directions. It was a pretty area and one I could imagine us revisiting for a quiet picnic lunch.

Nick stepped behind me, wound his arms around my waist and rested his chin on top of my head.

"If there weren't people around, I'd take you here. I missed you last night, babe."

He spun me in his arms, lowered his head and captured my lips in a knee weakening kiss. Desire cascaded over every inch of my body, I found myself wanting him desperately.

When he lifted his head, releasing my mouth, I gazed into his eyes.

"I want you, Nick."

"Home it is then." Grasping my hand, Nick led me the short distance to the truck and held the door open while I climbed in.

When he slid behind the wheel, he reached over and claimed my lips once again. He was like a man whose thirst couldn't be quenched when it came to us kissing.

I sighed when he drew away to start up the engine and rested my hand on his knee.

***

12 Months Later

Nick's parents – Rebecca and Walter had visited regularly over the past six months, the last couple of times they'd accepted mum and dad's offer to stay with them to give Nick and I more privacy. Not that either of us would have minded them staying with us.

They were lovely people and Nick's brother, Stuart, although like Nick in looks was a universe away from him in nature.

Where Nick was salt of the earth, loyal, serious, almost gruff at times; Stuart appeared to be one who lived life to the full and had an eye for the ladies.

It was obvious Nick and his parents had issued a warning where I was concerned, he was always careful to treat me as Nick's lady.

All three were currently in Longreach, leaving their property in the capable hands of their staff.

While Rebecca and Walter were staying with my parents, Stuart was visiting with a lady friend who had moved to Longreach for work.

As Nick drove towards my parent's home, I reflected on the past year….

Brutus was now a yearling who was showing more than a passing interest in females of his own species. Although he still came running when I called, he was only content to stay for a few pats and a kiss on the nose before heading back to his harem. He was now at an age where sperm production could begin and dad was in the process of having him tested.

My sanctuary – EmmaNick Farm was now up and functioning. On site was a three bedroom log home where managers – Alastair and his wife, Cindy resided with their two children – Clementine aged 12 and Peter aged 10.

The children were wonderful with the various animals, especially the rescued dogs and cats. Their gentle touch with those who had previously been abused, was reassuring and healing. Two dogs and a cat had found a permanent home with the family and they also played a role in the rehabilitation of their abused species.

I'd moved in with Nick three months earlier so although my days were spent caring for the animals, my nights were spent in his arms. Alistair and Rebecca also had the assistance of two night managers who each worked a roster of four on and four off.

One large barn was divided in half, orphaned calves from dad and Nick's properties in one half, sheep and goats in the other. A door led out to a secured pasture where they could frolic during the day. When the children weren't in school, they loved feeding and running around with the babies.

Another barn housed dogs in large kennels with runs on the ground floor, cats on the upper floor. Still another housed rabbits, chickens, possums and all manner of wildlife.

The stables could cope with up to six horses at a time and Nick had employed a man who specialized in the rehabilitation of abused horses to work with these sorry beasts.

Every facility was climate controlled and when the weather had been unbearably hot, we'd brought the animals into the cool of the inside.

Nick grumbled I was spoiling them to the point I'd have trouble with them when it came time to leave, but he wouldn't have had it any other way. They were animals which had begun life hard, it was time they were pampered.

The entire setup was everything I'd dreamed it would be.

***

Nick clutched my hand as we entered mum and dad's home. The house was quiet but laughter from out the back could be heard. We made our way through the house and when we stepped outside, we were greeted by a sea of people.

Dad and Nick's father were chatting while they stood at the barbeque, steaks sizzled, beers were in hands.

All the ranch hands from both properties were in attendance and some men I knew from Walter's property up in Winton. Friends of ours from town mingled, even Alistair, Rebecca and their children were present.

Nick shouted out hello before I could open my mouth to ask what the hell was going on. Everyone spun our way and quieted.

Nick moved to stand in front of me, took both of my hands in his and dropped to one knee.

"Oh my God," I whispered.

Nick placed a finger to my lips and I didn't attempt to say another word. He took my hand back into his.

"Emma, it's one year today since you steamrolled into my life thanks to Nero and his imitation of Houdini. I think we can both agree, it wasn't a pleasant first encounter. I had never met such a frustrating woman; your strange ideas were mind boggling and you wanted to put my quad bike in the river. I'd muttered to Nero all the way home, blaming him for putting me in your path. I'd grumbled about you being some new-age hippie, wannabe grazier who knew nothing about the outback and stock. I mean, who the hell kisses a bull on the nose? A two tonne bull you'd never met before! When I saw you do that, I thought I needed my eyes tested because I must have been seeing things."

He sucked in a deep breath before continuing.

"Then, I saw you were hurt and over the following few days, I witnessed a vulnerable, caring, giving side of you. Despite the fact you could barely walk, you still insisted on caring for Brutus because you said he needed you and you weren't going to let him down."

Nick stopped and wiped a hot tear from my cheek with his handkerchief.

"Over the past year, I've watched your excitement, enthusiasm, willingness to listen and learn. Your energy and compassion as you cared for different animals which needed help. You have opened your heart to the people of Longreach and I think we have all learned as much from you as you have from us. I've accepted your belief that animals do indeed have feelings, they do suffer loneliness and grief. You have stolen my heart, Emma. I love you more than life itself and I would go to the ends of the earth to make your dreams come true. So, Emmalynne Jacqueline Peters, will you make my dream come true and marry me?"

Tears streamed over my cheeks and I heard a few sniffles from people nearby. I gazed into Nick's eyes which were full of hope and promise.

There was no hesitation, I knew where my heart belonged. "Yes. Yes. YES!"

Nick whopped, stood, swept me into his arms and kissed me while he spun me around.

Clapping, cheering and whistling erupted from family and friends.

Nick placed me back on the ground, dug in his pocket, lifted my left hand and slid on a stunning silver ring which had a midnight blue sapphire surrounded by diamonds. After I admired it for a moment, I lifted my head and locked eyes with Nick.

"I love you so much, Nicholas Graham Johnson."

Nick smiled. "I know."

A sensual kiss followed before my fiancé wrapped an arm around my waist and yelled, "Let's get this party started, where's the champagne?"

I laughed before the hugging and kissing from family and friends began.

***

My life now?

Retiring last year and meeting Nick was the best thing to ever happen to me. People in Longreach knew who I was, what I'd done, but not once had they treated me any differently to one of their own.

The month of March had a special place in my heart and would always be my favourite of the year.

It was the month I'd met the man I was now deeply in love with.

The month my entire life had changed.

The month in which Nick had proposed and.....

I had no doubt it would be the month we would marry the following year.

THE END

Author Links

Blog: http://susanhorsnell.com

Web: http://www.susanhorsnellromanceauthor.com/

Facebook:
https://www.facebook.com/susanhorsnellroma
nceauthor/

Bookbub:
https://www.bookbub.com/profile/susan-
horsnell

Newsletter: http://bit.ly/2t5INNB

Printed in Australia
AUHW021513271021
354375AU00059B/459